"What exactly did Dad say to you?"

Colby's gaze touched hers, then withdrew. "That you'd fallen head over heels in love with me. And that's a quote."

"What?" Valerie said incredulously.

Colby gave an indifferent shrug. "That's what he says. But eventually he's going to have to realize you're not the kind of woman I intend to marry."

"Believe me, Dr. Winston," she murmured, "you have nothing to worry about."

"Still, I'm afraid you'll have to say something to him."

"Why can't we just let the whole thing drop? By tomorrow he'll have forgotten all about it."

Colby shook his head. "That's not likely. He asked me to bring in a preacher so we could be married at his bedside."

Valerie couldn't help it—she burst out laughing.

Dear Reader,

I'm thrilled and excited that you're reading the ORCHARD VALLEY trilogy. These three books—*Valerie, Stephanie* and *Norah*—come straight from my heart.

I was born and raised in Yakima, Washington, which is often referred to as the apple capital of the world. Huge orchards spread out across the Yakima Valley, and the scent of flowering apple trees fills the air each spring. How well I remember their beauty—and the dread of a late-spring freeze!

I've loosely based Orchard Valley on Yakima and on the small town of Port Orchard, where my husband and I moved several years ago to raise our family. Although I've situated Orchard Valley in Oregon, it could be any small town, anywhere in the United States or Canada. Any small town where there's a sense of community, where people help each other, where neighbors become friends. I hope I've succeeded in capturing that wonderful small-town feeling.

The three sisters in these books are reunited because of a family crisis. There's nothing like the threat of losing someone we love to help us recognize our real values and appreciate our families, our roots. I hope that (like me!) you'll weep with Valerie as she discovers what really matters in life and that you'll sympathize with Stephanie as she deals with her past. And I'm sure you'll cheer with Norah as she meets her match!

I'd be delighted to learn your reactions to the ORCHARD VALLEY trilogy. (In fact, I *always* love hearing from my readers!) You can write to me at P.O. Box 1458, Port Orchard, Washington 98366.

Sincerely,

Debbie Macomber

VALERIE
Debbie Macomber

Harlequin Books

TORONTO • NEW YORK • LONDON
AMSTERDAM • PARIS • SYDNEY • HAMBURG
STOCKHOLM • ATHENS • TOKYO • MILAN
MADRID • WARSAW • BUDAPEST • AUCKLAND

To Dr. John T. and Kelly Dykstra—
in grateful appreciation for their continued
support of the American Heart Association

ISBN 0-373-03232-3

Harlequin Romance first edition November 1992

VALERIE

Copyright © 1992 by Debbie Macomber.

Printed in U.S.A.

CHAPTER ONE

"NORAH? Is that you?" Valerie Bloomfield's voice rose expectantly. She'd been trying to reach her sister for the past hour with no success.

"Valerie, where are you? You don't sound right."

"That's because I'm somewhere over Nebraska—at least I think it's Nebraska." It was difficult to tell thirty thousand feet above the ground. "How's Dad?"

Norah hesitated and that slight pause sent Valerie's worry escalating into panic. "Norah..." she began.

"He's doing as well as can be expected."

"Did you tell him I'm on my way?" Valerie had been in the middle of a New York business meeting when she received the message. Her youngest sister had called the Houston office first, and they'd passed on the news of her father's heart attack. Valerie had left immediately, catching the first available flight to Oregon.

"Dad knows you're coming."

"Were you able to get hold of Steff?"

Norah's answering sigh signaled her frustration. "Yes, but it took forever and my Italian is nonexistent. She's planning to catch whatever she can out of Rome, but she has to get there first—she's in some little village right now. It might take her a couple of days. The connection was bad and I couldn't understand everything she said. Apparently there's some sort of transportation strike going on. But she's doing her best...."

Valerie's sympathies went out to Stephanie, the middle Bloomfield sister. She must be frantic, stuck halfway across the world and desperate to find a way home.

"When will you arrive?" Norah asked anxiously.

"The plane's scheduled to land at six-ten."

"Do you want me to meet you? I could—"

"No," Valerie interrupted. She didn't think it was a good idea for Norah to leave their father. "I've already ordered a car. It shouldn't take me more than forty minutes once I land, so don't worry about me."

"But the hospital's an hour's drive from the airport. You shouldn't even try to make it in less."

It generally did take a full hour, but Valerie had every intention of getting there a lot sooner. "I should be at the hospital somewhere around seven," she said evasively.

"I'll see you then," Norah said, sounding resigned.

"Don't worry, kid, everything's going to be all right."

"Just be careful, will you?" Norah pleaded. "Having you involved in an accident won't help Dad any."

"I'll be careful," Valerie promised, smiling at her sister's words. Trust Norah to take the practical approach. After a brief farewell, Valerie replaced the telephone in the slot in front of her.

Closing her eyes, she tried to rest, but the effort was useless. Her thoughts seemed to be traveling at the speed of light, zooming through her head, quickening her pulse.

Her father was dying. Her dear, precious father... His hold on life was precarious, and the burning need to get to him as quickly as possible drove her like nothing she'd ever experienced.

Sleep was out of the question. Valerie bent down for her purse, rummaging through it until she found the antacid tablets. She popped one in her mouth and chewed it with a vengeance.

No sooner had she swallowed the chalky tablet than she reached for a roll of the hard candies she always carried with her. Two years earlier she'd given up smoking, and sucking on hard candy had helped her through the worst of the nicotine withdrawal. If she'd ever needed a cigarette, it was now. Her nerves were stretched to the breaking point.

Dear heaven, not her father, too. Valerie was only beginning to come to grips with her mother's death. Grace Bloomfield had died of cancer almost four years ago, and the grief had shaken Valerie's well-ordered life. She'd buried her anguish in her work; the biggest strides in her career with CHIPS, a Texas-based computer software company, had come in the past few years. She'd risen quickly up the corporate ladder, until she was the youngest executive on the management team.

Her father had reacted similarly to Grace's death. Working too many hours, driving himself too hard. Norah had tried to tell her, but Valerie hadn't paid attention. She should have done something, anything, to get their father to slow down, to relax and enjoy life. He should have retired years before; he could be traveling, seeing exotic places, meeting with old friends and making new ones. In the years since her mother's death, Valerie had been able to convince her father to leave Orchard Valley only once and that had been a two-week trip to Italy to visit Steffie.

And now he was fighting for his life in a hospital.

Valerie hadn't said anything to him because... well, because they were so much alike. David Bloomfield was working out his grief the same way she was. Valerie couldn't very well criticize him for something she was doing herself.

Before she knew it, she'd chomped her way through two rolls of candy and another of antacid tablets.

When the plane landed, Valerie was the first one off, scurrying with her carryon bag down the concourse to the rental car agency. Within fifteen minutes, she was on the freeway heading east toward Orchard Valley.

Heading toward home.

NORAH WAS RIGHT; it took Valerie longer than forty minutes to reach Orchard Valley Hospital. She was there in forty-five. She claimed the first available parking space, unconcerned about whether the rental car would be towed away. What did concern her was seeing her father.

Norah was standing in the hospital lobby when Valerie walked through the double glass doors. Her sister, looking drawn and pale, was visibly relieved by her presence. "Oh, Valerie," she said, covering her mouth with one hand. "Oh, Valerie... I'm so glad you're here."

"Dad?" Valerie's throat closed up. If her cantankerous father had had the audacity to die before she arrived, she'd never forgive him. The thought made her realize how mentally and physically drained this ordeal had left her.

"He's resting comfortably...for now."

Valerie hugged her sister. Norah looked dreadful, her stylish shoulder-length blond hair brushed away from her face as if her hands had swept it behind her ears countless times. Her blue eyes, normally so clear and bright, were red-rimmed from tears and lack of sleep.

Valerie hadn't had much rest herself, but she was still running on adrenaline. She wouldn't collapse until after she'd had a chance to spend some time with her father.

"What exactly happened?" she asked as they hurried to the elevator. Their shoes made sharp, clicking sounds against the polished linoleum floor, sounds that reminded Valerie of similar visits almost four years ago, when her mother was dying. She remembered similar nighttime walks down these silent corridors. She hadn't been to this hospital since. The memories overwhelmed her now, tearing at the facade of her poise.

"After dinner, Dad went out onto the porch," Norah began, her voice quavering.

As far back as Valerie could remember, after the evening meal her parents had adjourned for coffee to the sweeping front porch of their large colonial home. They'd sat together on the old wicker chairs, sometimes holding hands and whispering like teenagers. Valerie was never sure what they discussed, but she'd learned early on not to interrupt her parents then. In the winters, they'd sat in front of the basalt fireplace in her father's den, but spring, summer and as far into the autumn as possible, it was the porch.

"I should have known something was wrong then," Norah continued. "Dad hasn't sat on the porch much since Mom's been gone. After dinner he generally goes right into his office and works on the bookkeeping."

The guilt Valerie experienced was crushing. Norah had repeatedly told her how hard their father was driving himself. She should have listened, should have demanded he hire an assistant, take a vacation, *something*. She should have stepped in. As the oldest, she felt responsible.

His heart was weak and had been since a bout of rheumatic fever in his early thirties. By all accounts he should have died then, but a young nurse's devotion had pulled him through. The nurse was Grace Johnson, who became David's wife, and Valerie, Stephanie and Norah's mother.

"I brought him out a cup of coffee," Norah went on, "and he looked up at me and smiled. He...he seemed to think I was Mom."

"Was he in terrible pain?"

Norah bit her lower lip. "Yes, he must have been. He was so pale... Only he was too proud to admit it. I asked him what was wrong, but he wouldn't answer. He just kept saying he was ready."

"Ready for what?"

Norah looked away, pain etched in her eyes. "Ready to die."

"Die," Valerie cried, "that's ridiculous. If there was ever a man who had something to live for, it's Dad. Good grief, he's worked hard all his life! Now, it's time to reap the fruits of his labors, to enjoy his family, to travel, to—"

"You don't need to convince me," Norah said quietly as they reached the third floor and stepped out of the elevator. The Coronary Care nurses' station stood directly in front of them. Norah walked to the counter.

"Betty, would you tell Dr. Winston my sister's arrived?"

"Right away," the plump matron replied. Even if the other woman hadn't been wearing a crisp white uniform, Valerie would have known Betty was a nurse. The signs were all there. She appeared to be gentle, compassionate—and practical. No-nonsense. Valerie recognized the look because the other woman shared it with Norah. And with their mother...

Valerie had to suppress a sudden smile at the memory of her youngest sister lining up dolls in her bed and sticking thermometers in their mouths. She'd fussed over them like an anxious mother, bandaging their limbs and offering reassurances and comfort.

Norah came by this temperament naturally, Valerie supposed, since their mother had been the same. Although she'd given up her hospital job when she married David Bloomfield, Grace continued to nurture those around her all her life. It had been her gift. It was Norah's gift, too.

"Who's Dr. Winston?" Valerie asked. She'd never heard of him before; he must be a recent addition to the hospital staff. But the last thing their father needed at a time like this was some hayseed family practitioner. He should be in a major hospital with the best heart surgeon available!

"Dr. Winston's been wonderful," Norah returned, her eyes lighting up briefly. "If it hadn't been for Colby, we would've lost Dad in the first twelve hours."

"Colby?" The doctor was named after a cheese? This didn't sound promising.

"I don't know what I would have done without him," Norah said. "I wasn't sure what to do with Dad at first. I guessed he was in a lot of pain, but I knew he'd object if I called for an Aid Car. He'd argue with me and that would have made matters even worse if it was his heart, the way I suspected."

"So you phoned Dr. Winston?"

"Yes. Luckily I was able to reach him, and he drove out, pretending to drop in out of the blue. He knew the minute he saw Dad that it was a heart attack. He sat down on the porch and had a cup of coffee with him."

"He drank coffee while our father was suffering a heart attack?" Valerie wasn't finding this doctor too endearing.

"I believe it was what saved Dad's life," Norah said, her eyes flashing a protest. "Dr. Winston was able to convince Dad to go to the hospital voluntarily. It wasn't until he'd been admitted that he suffered the worst of the attack. If he'd been at home arguing, no one could have done anything to save him."

"Oh." That took some of the heat out of Valerie's argument. She suspected she was looking for someone to blame. It would help ease her guilt for having ignored Norah's concerns about their father.

The door Betty had disappeared behind opened then, and a tall dark-haired man walked toward them, his eyes serious. Valerie couldn't help noticing how attractive he was. In fact, the man had movie-star good looks, but good looks that had nothing insipid or soft about them.

"Hello," he said, his voice deep and resonant. "I'm Dr. Winston." He held out his hand.

"Valerie Bloomfield," she replied briskly, placing her hand in his. She'd always been taught it was impolite to stare, but she couldn't stop herself. Her father's physician didn't look much older than her own twenty-eight years. "Excuse me," she said, not glancing at Norah, who would, she suspected, immediately leap to Dr. Winston's defense. "I don't mean to be rude—but how old are you?"

"Valerie," Norah groaned under her breath.

"I just want to know how long he's been practicing medicine. Good grief, Norah, this is our *father.*"

"It's quite all right," Dr. Winston said, with a reassuring smile at Norah. "If David was my father I'd have a few questions myself. I'm thirty-six."

Valerie found it hard to believe, but she couldn't very well insist on seeing his birth certificate. Besides, her thoughts were muddled and she was exhausted. Now wasn't the time to question his qualifications. "How's my father?" she asked instead.

"He's resting."

"When will I be able to see him?"

"I'd rather you didn't go in right away."

"What do you mean?" Valerie snapped. "I've flown all the way across the country to be with my father. He needs me! Certainly I should be able to go to him."

"It wouldn't be a good idea just now. He's sleeping for the first time in nearly twenty hours and I don't want anything to disturb him."

"I think you should wait," Norah seconded, as if she feared Valerie might be on the verge of making a scene.

Valerie sighed; her sister was right. "Of course I'll wait. It's just that I'm anxious."

"I understand," Dr. Winston said. But he spoke without emotion. He led them to a waiting room not far from the nurses' station. Two well-worn couches faced each other, and several outdated magazines littered the coffee table that rested between them. A coffeepot stood in one corner, with powdered creamer and an ample supply of disposable cups.

Norah sat first, covering her mouth in an effort to hide a wide yawn.

"How long have you been here?" Valerie asked, realizing even before she asked that Norah had stayed at the hospital since that first night. Her youngest sister was exhausted, physically and emotionally. "Listen, kid, you go on home and get some rest. I'll hold down the fort for a while."

Norah grinned sheepishly. "I used to hate it when you called me kid, but I don't anymore."

"Why not?" Valerie asked softly, resisting the urge to brush a stray curl from her sister's forehead. She wasn't the maternal type, but she felt protective toward Norah, wanting to ease the weight of her burden.

"You can call me kid anytime you like because that's exactly the way I feel, like a child whose world has been tossed upside down. I'm scared, Val, really scared. We almost lost him—we still could."

"I know," Valerie whispered, briefly hugging her. Norah had suffered through the worst of the nightmare, facing the fear alone, not knowing from one minute to the next if their father was going to live or die.

"Valerie's right," Dr. Winston added. "There's nothing you can do here. Go home and rest. I promise I'll call you if there's any change."

Norah rubbed a hand across her eyes and nodded. "I'll take a shower and try to sleep for a couple of hours. That's all I need. Two, maybe three hours."

Valerie wondered if Norah was too exhausted to drive by herself. But Dr. Winston must have had the same concerns.

"We'll phone for a cab from the nurses' station. I don't want you driving like this." He placed his arm around Norah's shoulders, apparently intending to

walk her to the elevator. As they left, he turned to
Valerie. "I'll be back in a few minutes."

While he was away, Valerie poured herself a cup of
coffee. There was no telling how long the pot had been
sitting there. The coffee was black and thick and
strong, just the way she needed it.

The urge for a cigarette was nearly overwhelming,
so when Dr. Winston returned to the room she looked
up at him and automatically asked, "I don't suppose
you have any hard candy with you?"

"I beg your pardon?"

"Mints, anything like that." She was pacing the
room, holding her coffee cup between both hands.

"I'm afraid not. Would you like me to see if I could
get you some?"

Valerie dismissed his offer with a shake of her head.
He was polite to a fault. The first thing she'd done had
been to insult him, question his competence, and he'd
taken it all with a smile.

"Please, tell me about my father."

They sat and for the next fifteen minutes, Dr. Winston explained exactly what had happened to her
father's heart. He did his best to outline it in lay-
man's terms, but much of what he said was beyond
Valerie's comprehension. She'd never been comfortable with medical matters. Her mother and Norah had
always dealt with those. For her part, Valerie hated
anything to do with hospitals or doctors. She detested
being sick herself, and knew her father felt the same
way.

"There's one underlying problem that needs to be
dealt with, however."

"Yes?" Valerie asked, hating the way her voice betrayed her concern. Any show of weakness distressed her. If she'd ever needed to be strong, it was now, for everyone's sake, including her own. She was the oldest, and the others would rely on her.

"Your father's lost his will to live."

"But that's ridiculous," she cried, battling the urge to argue with him. "My father's life is brimming over, it's so full. Why he's—"

"Lost without your mother," Dr. Winston finished simply.

Valerie bolted to her feet and resumed pacing. What Dr. Winston said was absolutely true; she had to admit it. Her father had been crushed under the load of grief, and while Valerie and her two sisters struggled to regain their own balance, their father had been slowly destroyed by his loss.

"What can we do?" she asked, trying to swallow her fears and her guilt.

"Support him, give him your love. The only thing keeping him alive now is his desire to see all three of his daughters before he dies."

"But... Okay, then don't let him know I'm here." It was the obvious solution. And if that was what it took to keep him alive, she was willing to play a little game of hide-and-seek. Norah could make up a series of excuses. No, forget Norah, Valerie mused bleakly. Her youngest sister couldn't tell a lie without blushing.

"How well do you lie?" she asked, thinking fast.

Dr. Winston blinked. "I beg your pardon?"

"We can't let my father know I've arrived. And that means lying to him."

"Miss Bloomfield—"

"Ms."

"Whatever," he said, sounding impatient with her for the first time. "We aren't going to be able to fool your father. Norah talked to him shortly after you phoned from...where was it? Nebraska? He knows you caught a flight out of New York. No one's going to make him believe something more important came up that's kept you from him."

"Steffie!" Valerie cried. "When Norah spoke to her, she said something about a transportation strike."

"Yes, but these are only stop-gap measures. Your father feels there's nothing worthwhile left to live for. He talks about your mother constantly, almost as though he's waiting to join her. We need something concrete that'll give him the will to fight, to hold on to life."

Again Valerie knew the doctor was right, but her confused brain was having trouble assimilating the most basic details, let alone something as complex as this.

"He's all we have," she whispered, shaking her head despondently. "Surely he realizes that."

"Yes, but at the same time, he believes you have one another."

"We don't get along that well," Valerie told him insistently. "And we have nothing in common. Steffie's a crazy woman who flies off to Europe to study the Italian Renaissance, and Norah's main goal in life is to become another Clara Barton. We don't even *look* alike.'' Valerie was grasping at weak excuses, and she knew it. Anything she could think of to enlist Dr. Winston's help in keeping her father alive.

"You don't need to convince me, Valerie," he told her gently. "I'll do everything I can to see that your father regains his health and lives to a ripe old age."

Blinking away tears, Valerie nodded, reminding herself once again that she was the oldest of David Bloomfield's daughters. In a crisis everyone looked to her; she was the one who needed a cool, decisive head, who couldn't let her emotions dictate her reactions.

But it was different this time.

The man in that hospital bed, barely holding on to life, was her father, the man she idolized and loved beyond reason. Her emotions were so close to the surface that the force of them frightened her.

"I'd—I'd like to see him as soon as possible. Please." She'd grovel if necessary. She *had* to be with her father. "I won't make the least bit of noise, I promise." The last thing she wanted to do was disturb his rest. Somehow, though, she had to reassure herself that he was still alive. She'd never been more frightened.

Dr. Winston hesitated. "Wait here, I'll be right back."

He returned a few moments later. "He's awake and asking for you."

Valerie was so eager that she nearly vaulted out of the room, but Dr. Winston stopped her. "Before you go to your father, let me prepare you for what you're going to see." He spent the next five minutes explaining the different medical devices used to monitor his patient's heart. He explained how the small electrodes on her father's chest detected the electrical impulses that signal the heart's activity. He warned her about the tubes going in and out of his body.

However, nothing he said could have prepared Valerie for what she saw. Her father was connected to so many devices that it hardly seemed possible they could all be flowing into one body. His face was ashen, so pale and bloodless that his skin seemed iridescent. His eyes, which had always seemed to spark with vitality, revealed no emotion, only a weariness that was soul deep.

"Oh, Daddy," Valerie whispered, fighting tears. She locked her fingers around his hand, careful not to disturb the intravenous needle.

"Valerie...so pleased you're here...at last."

"Where else would I be?" she asked, forcing a smile. With the back of her other hand, she brushed a stray tear from her cheek.

"She's beautiful, isn't she?" her father said, apparently talking to Dr. Winston, who hovered in the doorway. "Only what did you do to your hair?"

"Do you like it?" Valerie asked, rallying somewhat, surprised he'd even noticed that she'd changed the style. "I had it cut." The new look was short and frothy.

"She's got the temper to go with that red hair, you know."

Her father was speaking to Colby Winston again.

"My hair isn't even close to being red," she argued, annoyed by the doctor's struggle not to grin. "It's auburn."

"Looks like you haven't combed it in a month," her father mumbled.

"Dad, this is the latest style. I'll have you know I paid good money for this."

"In that case, you should demand a refund." His voice was weak, and speaking had clearly drained him of what little energy he possessed.

"Dad," Valerie whispered, doing her best to disguise her concern. "Instead of complaining about my hair, you should rest."

He seemed too weak to reply. He closed his eyes and sighed audibly.

"I'm going to leave you for a little while," Valerie said. "But I'll be right outside the door, so if you want to tell me how much you like my hair and beg my forgiveness, then all you need to do is signal the nurse." Dr. Winston had explained earlier that she'd be allowed to visit her father five minutes out of every hour, depending on how well he was doing.

His responding smile was barely discernible.

"Rest now, Daddy. I'm here."

Dr. Winston's hand was at her elbow directing her out of the glass-enclosed cubicle.

"Doc?" Her father's voice had a sense of urgency.

"What is it, David?"

"She's the one I was telling you about. You remember what I said, don't you?"

"Yes. Now don't you worry about a thing."

"Her hair doesn't generally look like a rag doll's."

"Daddy!" Valerie hadn't a clue what was taking place between the two men but she wasn't going to idly stand by and let them insult her.

"This way," Colby Winston said, directing her from the Coronary Care Unit.

"What was that all about?" Valerie demanded the instant they were out of earshot.

"I'm not sure I know what you mean," he said without meeting her gaze.

Valerie wasn't fooled. There was definitely something going on, and she wanted to know what. She'd been in business too long to allow questionable remarks to slip past her unchallenged.

"What did Dad mean, I'm 'the one'?"

Dr. Winston's eyes still refused to meet hers. "While we—your father and I—were talking earlier, he voiced a few concerns about his daughters."

"Yes?" Valerie pressed. Making an effort to appear nonchalant and relaxed, she walked over to the coffeepot and lifted it to him in silent invitation.

Dr. Winston shook his head and Valerie refilled her own paper cup. "So, what did Dad have to say about us girls?" she asked softly.

"He's very proud of all three of you."

"Naturally. We're his children. What I'd like to know is what he meant when he said I was 'the one.'"

"Yes, well…" He walked away from her and stood gazing out the window into the night sky.

"Come now, Doctor, I'm a mature woman and this is my father. I'm sure if I pressed him he'd tell me." They both knew that coercing her father was out of the question; nevertheless, it was an effective ploy. Dr. Winston went to the coffeepot and filled a cup, even though he'd refused one moments earlier.

"It seems he's the most worried about you."

"Me?" Valerie cried. Of the three girls, she was by far the most stable. She was not only gainfully employed, but living on her own. For heaven's sake, she was the only one with any investments! "That makes no sense at all."

"Yes, well . . ."

"Why is he worried about me? Furthermore, why didn't he say something to *me* instead of talking it over with you?"

"There are any number of reasons—"

"Just tell me what he said," Valerie interrupted impatiently.

"Your father seems to think—"

"Yes?" she prompted when he hesitated.

"That you should be married."

Valerie couldn't restrain her laughter. It shot out of her, like bubbles from a champagne bottle.

"In fact," Colby continued grimly, "your father seems to think you should be married to me."

CHAPTER TWO

"MARRIED TO YOU?" Valerie echoed, her laughter fading suddenly. Dr. Colby Winston! She'd never heard anything so preposterous in her life. She had no intention of marrying *anyone* within the foreseeable future. There was simply no room for a man in her life. She wasn't much of a romantic; even when she was younger and in college, she hadn't dated much. Her father knew all that, and he'd never seemed particularly worried about it. This latest revelation shocked her nearly as much as Norah's call.

"I don't think there's any reason to be too concerned," Colby said, his voice gentle as though he understood that his announcement had unsettled her. Generally she was better at disguising her emotions.

"This sort of delusion isn't unheard of in heart patients," he continued. "As I said, I certainly don't think you need to concern yourself."

"You mean your patients generally try to marry you off?"

"No." He smoothed his tie as if he needed something to do with his hands. "Your father fully expects to die. It's what he wants, and deep down he'd feel better about leaving the three of you behind if at least one of you was married. Your father and I are friends and it's only natural that he'd attempt to pair me up with one of his daughters."

"It should have been Norah. She seems more your type."

His smile was fleeting. "Perhaps, but it's your name he repeatedly mentions."

"Then apparently I'm the one," Valerie said, not realizing what she was saying until the words had left her mouth. "I mean—" She stopped abruptly.

"I know exactly what you mean," Colby assured her. "I don't think we have to take any of this seriously."

"Oh, I agree. That would be foolish in the extreme."

"Maybe your father feels you should marry first because you're the oldest," Colby ventured.

"Maybe," Valerie agreed after a moment. But something inside her suggested that wasn't the sole reason. She tucked her arms around her stomach and inhaled deeply, hoping to breathe in a bit of calm and sense.

"I wouldn't have said anything," Colby said, "but I thought it was best to air this. If he mentions marriage again, my feeling is we should go along with him, at least for now."

"Go along with him? You've got to be kidding." Valerie could barely believe her ears.

Colby shrugged. "I'm sure you know your father better than I do," he muttered. "He's as stubborn as they come. Don't lie, but whenever he mentions the subject of... marriage, if he does, take the route of least resistance, then try to channel the conversation in a different direction.''

"I'm not going to give my father any false hopes. Or for that matter, you." She added the last part coyly and was rewarded when she saw him swallow tightly— as if he were swallowing his irritation. An angry spark momentarily leaped into his dark eyes, but was quickly quelled.

Sitting down, Valerie rummaged through her purse for a spare roll of antacid tablets. Her stomach ached and she was weary to her very bones.

Colby ignored her, although he made no move to go. The preoccupied look on his face suggested that he had something else to say; he seemed to be searching for words.

Valerie considered what Colby had told her. If she ever decided to marry—*if*—she'd settle down with someone who possessed the same drive, the same will to succeed, as she did. A man who knew where he was going, who'd set his sights high. Not some well-meaning small-town doctor.

She'd marry a man like Rowdy Cassidy.

The name sprang into her mind with a suddenness that shocked her.

Until that moment, Valerie didn't realize how deeply she admired her employer. Rowdy had started his computer software business out of a friend's garage fifteen years earlier. He'd built the company into one of the most successful in the country. Although he'd earned more money than he could possibly spend in a lifetime, he continued to work ten- and twelve-hour days, demanding as much of his staff as he did of himself.

"It might, uh, help matters if you were involved with someone," Colby said in a casual voice. Valerie found his nonchalant tone a bit exaggerated, which for some reason made her suspect that he *wasn't* "involved with someone."

"I'm not in a relationship at the moment, but I might be soon," she told him. Valerie and Rowdy—a couple. Odd that she'd never thought of him in romantic terms before. He'd be the perfect husband for her. She liked him and respected him, as a man and a professional. Rowdy had hand-picked her for his management team because he believed in her abilities.

In retrospect, she realized Rowdy had sought out her company on several occasions. Several private meetings, in fact. But she'd been so absorbed in proving herself worthy of his faith that she hadn't guessed he might hold any personal feelings for her.

For months she'd been blind to what was right in front of her. Not that she was entirely to blame, though. Rowdy wasn't exactly a heart-throb kind of guy. Oh, he was handsome enough, with his rugged cowboy looks, but his brusque, outspoken manner didn't encourage romantic aspirations. As far as she knew, he'd never dated anyone seriously, at least not in the years she'd worked for him.

For that matter, Valerie wasn't any expert on falling in love, either. She'd dismissed the possibility of romance in her own life; it was fine for her sisters and schoolfriends, but not for her. There'd always been too much she wanted to do, too much to strive for. Too much to achieve before settling down in a permanent relationship.

"I'm afraid I don't understand," Colby said, breaking into her thoughts. At her blank look, he elaborated. "You said you weren't involved with someone *yet,* but you will be soon. I may be overstepping my bounds here, but I wouldn't advise you to invent a phony relationship. Your father would see through that in a minute."

"I agree. I wouldn't even attempt anything so foolish. But there's a man I work with, and, well, it seems natural for the two of us to...get involved."

Dr. Winston looked so relieved that she might have been offended if she hadn't been warmed by the newly risen hope of a romance with Rowdy Cassidy.

"I've given your father something to help him rest," Colby went on. "He should sleep through the night without a problem, so if you want to drive home and join your sister—"

"No," Valerie interrupted quickly. "I won't leave Dad. I realize I can't see him yet, but I want to be here...in case anything happens. It's important to me."

"I understand."

Valerie was grateful. "Thank you."

He nodded, then yawned, revealing for the first time his own fatigue. "I've left orders that I'm to be contacted the minute there's any change in his condition."

"I can't thank you enough for everything you've done."

"No thanks necessary. I'll talk to you in the morning."

Valerie smiled and sat down to leaf through a six-month-old news magazine. She'd just finished reading the letters to the editor when the nurse appeared, carrying a pillow and a blanket.

"Dr. Winston thought you might need these," she said, setting the bundle down next to Valerie.

It was a thoughtful thing to do, she mused later as she rested her head against the pillow and tucked the thin blanket around her shoulders. She felt a twinge of guilt, especially since she'd already decided to call in the country's top heart surgeon first thing in the morning.

By noon, it was unlikely that her father would still be a patient of Dr. Colby Winston's.

HE LIKED HER, Colby realized. He'd been prepared not to. Valerie Bloomfield was everything her father had claimed. Professional, astute and lively. But when it came to relationships, she was exactly the type of woman Colby made a point of avoiding.

He liked his women soft and feminine. He was looking for a wife, and David Bloomfield had somehow intuited that, or he wouldn't have dragged his eldest daughter into almost every conversation. But Colby didn't have a business executive in mind. He needed a helpmate, a woman who understood the never-ending demands of a doctor's work. A woman who'd understand the long hours, the emotional stress, the intrusions into his private life.

What he didn't need was a career-obsessed executive. Perhaps he was a bit outdated in his thinking. He certainly acknowledged that a woman had every right to pursue her own profession, to choose her own calling in life, but Colby was looking for a woman who'd make that calling *him*.

He had to admit it sounded selfish and egocentric to expect his wife to wrap her life around his. Nevertheless that was exactly what he wanted.

His own career was all-consuming; there weren't enough hours in the day to do everything that needed to be done. When he arrived home at night he wanted someone there to greet him, to offer comfort, serenity.

Sherry Waterman fit the bill perfectly. They'd been dating off and on for almost a year. Lately, it seemed, more off than on. Colby wasn't sure why he'd allowed his relationship with Sherry to taper off. He hadn't talked to her in nearly two weeks now—maybe longer. He didn't remember anymore. But he knew she'd be an ideal wife for him, and for that matter so would Norah Bloomfield. Yet he couldn't picture spending the rest of his life with either of them.

If he was going to analyze his lack of interest in both Sherry and Norah, then he might as well examine what it was he found so attractive about Valerie. Not the briefcase she carried with her like a second purse. Certainly not the way she popped antacid tablets, or the way she dressed in a sexless gray suit that disguised every feminine curve of her slender frame.

What appealed to him most was the contrast he read in her. Outwardly she appeared calm and collected, asking intelligent questions with the composure of someone inquiring about commonplace statistics instead of her father's chances of survival.

Colby hadn't been fooled. He noted how she gnawed on her lower lip even while her gaze steadily met his. Valerie had been badly shaken by the ordeal. There were depths of emotion in this woman, a real capacity for feeling that was—or so he guessed—usually kept hidden.

He also noticed the love in her eyes when he took her to see her father. He'd watched her struggle to keep the emotion at bay. Her fingers had trembled when they reached for her father's hand and her face had grown gentle. There was a strong bond between those two.

It hadn't been necessary to repeat David's comment about their marrying, and Colby wasn't sure why he had.

He suspected he'd been hoping to discover if she was involved with someone. Knowing that she was, or rather that she was about to be, should have reassured him. But it hadn't. If anything, he was more curious than ever.

NORAH'S ARRIVAL stirred Valerie into wakefulness early the following morning. She hadn't slept much, too exhausted and keyed up to let herself relax. Toward dawn she'd drifted into an uneasy slumber.

"How's Dad?" Norah asked, handing Valerie a white sack that contained breakfast.

"The same. I haven't been in to see him, but I've talked to the CCU staff several times." She'd paced the hospital corridor most of the night and as a result had received intermittent reports.

"He's been like this almost from the first, as though he's balancing on the edge of a cliff. He could fall either way."

"He'll live," Valerie said fervently, as though her determination was enough to keep him alive.

"I hope you're right."

"I am," Valerie returned, forcing her voice to remain confident.

"Oh, before I forget," Norah said, sitting opposite Valerie, "there were two messages on the answering machine when I got home last night. The first was from Mr. Cassidy at CHIPS. He's your boss, isn't he?"

Valerie nodded, opening the bag her sister had brought. She removed a warm croissant and cup of fresh coffee. The last time she could remember eating had been on the plane, and although the meal had looked fairly decent, she'd been too upset to feel very hungry.

"What'd Rowdy have to say?"

"Just that he'd heard about Dad's heart attack. He asked if there was anything he could do."

Valerie smiled to herself, pleased that Rowdy had taken a few moments from his busy schedule to call her. It seemed to confirm her thoughts of the night before; she was increasingly convinced that his interest in her was more than business.

"Who else phoned?" she asked, purposely turning her mind from Rowdy. There'd be plenty of time later to mull over her recent revelation.

"Steff."

"How's she doing?" Valerie asked before biting into the flaky croissant.

"Not very well, I'm afraid." Norah's shoulders slumped forward slightly. "She sounded almost desperate."

"I take it she hasn't left Italy yet?"

"She can't. Apparently the whole country's at a standstill. Like I told you, she's trapped in this tiny village a hundred miles or so outside of Rome. She'd gone there to spend a few days with a friend's family."

"Why doesn't she rent a car?"

"Apparently everyone else thought of the same thing. There's not a car to be had."

"What about her friends?"

"From what I understand, the people she's with don't have a car. She and her friend got a ride there from someone else, and everyone she knows is away on spring break. She sounded dreadful. I called her back, but she was out, so I left a message." Norah shook her head in frustration.

"What did you tell her?"

"That you'd arrived and...Dad's condition was stable." It was a small lie, but necessary, Valerie agreed, for their sister's peace of mind.

"I'll try to give her a call later," Valerie said, sipping the rapidly cooling coffee. She glanced at her watch and calculated the time difference between Oregon and Texas. If she phoned now she might be able to catch Rowdy. If he was in the office, she'd ask him to locate the best heart surgeon in the state.

The pay phone didn't afford Valerie much privacy, but that couldn't be helped. To her relief, she was immediately connected with her boss.

"Valerie," he said, his big voice booming over the wire. "Good to hear from you. How's your father?"

"We don't know yet. It could go either way."

"I'm sorry to hear that." Rowdy sounded genuinely concerned and again her heart warmed toward him. "If there's anything I can do, let me know."

"There is," Valerie said, lowering her voice in an effort not to be overheard. She glanced around to make sure no staff members were within earshot. "I need the name and phone number of the best heart surgeon in this state. No, make it the West Coast. Dad's too ill to be transferred to another hospital just yet, but the one here in Orchard Valley is small. I can't be sure he's getting the best possible care. I want to make other arrangements as soon as I can."

"Of course, I'll get right on it."

Not for the first time, Valerie felt a twinge of conscience. Colby Winston obviously cared about her father. If she hurt his professional pride by going behind his back, then she'd apologize. For now, though, her primary concern had to be her father, and if that meant offending a family friend, well, it couldn't be helped.

"How can I reach you at the hospital?" Rowdy asked.

Valerie gave him the number of the pay phone, which was the best she could do.

"I'll get back to you within the hour."

"I really appreciate this," Valerie told him.

A few moments later, she strolled into the waiting room where she'd left Norah. Colby had joined her and it struck Valerie a second time how perfect Norah would be for him.

Valerie should have been pleased by the idea. Excited, too. But she wasn't and she didn't know why.

Norah smiled at something Colby was saying, and Valerie realized with a small pang that her youngest sister was half in love with him already. If she could see it, then surely her father had, too. He was probably just confusing the two of them in his mind, Valerie reasoned, which was certainly understandable under the circumstances.

"Dad's doing about the same," Norah said when she became aware that Valerie had entered the room. "Colby was just in to see him."

"Good morning," he greeted her, smiling briefly.

"Morning." Feeling guilty, she couldn't meet his eyes.

"You may both take turns visiting your father if you'd like, but you can only stay five minutes, and I'd prefer that you waited an hour between visits."

"Fine," Valerie murmured. "Since I was with him last night, do you want to go first?" she asked Norah.

"All right."

Valerie assumed that Dr. Winston would go with her sister, but he stayed behind, pouring himself a cup of coffee from the freshly brewed pot. His back was to Valerie.

"Your father's going to require open-heart surgery," he said once he'd turned around to face her.

"Right now his heart's too weak to withstand the additional stress, but we're fast approaching a crisis point, and you and your sisters need to prepare yourselves."

"Here?" Valerie challenged. "And who'd perform the surgery?"

"I will— I *am* a qualified cardiovascular surgeon. And Orchard Valley has one of the best heart units in the state," Colby offered in a reassuring voice.

"I don't want *one* of the best, I want the *very* best! This is my *father* we're talking about." Valerie knew she sounded unreasonable, even rude, but her concern about David overrode all other considerations, including her embarrassment at misjudging Dr. Winston. Why had Norah never mentioned that the man was a heart surgeon? Still, it didn't matter; her father deserved the best-equipped facility and the best-trained specialist around. She spoke in a calmer voice. "If he needs surgery, then he'll have it, but not here. Not when there's a better hospital and more experienced..."

"Heart surgeons?" Colby finished for her.

She stiffened, wanting to avoid a confrontation and knowing it was impossible. "Exactly."

"You're welcome to a second opinion, Valerie. I'd be happy to review my credentials with you, as well."

Her arms cradled her middle. Her breakfast seemed to lie like a deadweight in her stomach.

Colby had begun to speak again. "Norah—"

"You already mentioned the possibility of open-heart surgery to Norah?" she flared, disliking the fact that he'd talked to her sister first.

He nodded. "Just now. While you were out."

That hurt her pride. She, after all, was the oldest, the decision maker, the strong one.

"If you'd like to talk to another specialist, I'd be happy to recommend several."

"That won't be necessary," Valerie returned stiffly, feeling like a traitor. "I'm having a friend get me the names of the top heart surgeons on the West Coast."

A vacuum of silence followed her words.

"I understand."

She glanced toward him, surprised not to hear any resentment in his voice.

"It isn't that we don't appreciate everything you've done," she rushed to explain. "Norah's told me several times that if it weren't for you, we'd have lost Dad that first night. I'm grateful, more than you'll ever know, but I want to stack the odds in Dad's favor, and if that means bringing in another surgeon, then I'll do it."

Her impassioned words were met with a cool but not unfriendly smile. "If David were my father I'd do the same. Don't worry, Valerie, you haven't offended me."

She was so relieved that she nearly sagged onto the sofa.

"Let me know who you want to call in and I'll be happy to confer with him."

"Thank you," she whispered. "Dad and Norah are right," she added, almost to herself.

"About what?" Colby asked on his way out the door.

She looked up, realizing he'd heard her. "You really are wonderful."

Their eyes met, all too briefly, but in those few seconds an odd understanding passed between them. It wasn't a look lovers would exchange, she thought, but one close friends would.

Norah returned from the five-minute visit with their father, pale and obviously distressed. Slowly she lowered herself onto the sofa, her hands gripped tightly together.

"Dad's not doing so well this morning?" Valerie ventured.

Norah nodded. "He's so weak...he's talking about dying and..." She paused, her light blue eyes glassy with tears.

"He isn't going to die," Valerie said vehemently, clenching her fists at her sides. She *refused* to let him die.

"He'd prefer if you and Steff and I were married, but that can't be helped now, he says. He told me he's sorry he won't be around to enjoy his grandchildren, but—"

"Norah," Valerie admonished briskly, "you didn't honestly listen to that garbage, did you? We can't allow him to talk like that."

"He seems to think you should marry Dr. Winston."

Valerie frowned. "So I heard. That just goes to show you how illogical he's become. If anyone should marry Colby Winston, it's you."

Norah lowered her eyes and an attractive shade of pink flowed into her cheeks. "Every female employee in the hospital's in love with Dr. Winston. Even the married ones have a crush on him. He's so strong, yet he's gentle and caring. I—I don't know what I would have done the last couple of days without Colby.''

"You really care about him, don't you?'' Valerie whispered, fighting down an unexpected sense of disappointment.

"I'm not in love with him—not exactly. I admire him the way everyone else does, and if he ever asked me out, I'd accept without thinking twice, but he hasn't.''

Valerie was sure she would. She paced the small room. "Damn, I need a cigarette,'' she blurted, uncertain what prompted the outburst—her father's apparent death wish or Norah's feelings for Colby Winston.

"I've been busy this morning myself,'' Valerie said, not looking at her sister. "I asked Rowdy Cassidy if he'd get us the name of the best heart surgeon on the West Coast. Dad's going to need the finest medical—"

Norah's head shot up. "You *what?*''

"Listen, if you're concerned about offending Colby, I've already spoken to him and he agrees we should get a second opinion.''

"But Colby teaches at Portland University. He's the best there is!''

"For Orchard Valley.'' Of that Valerie was confident, but there was a whole world Norah knew little or nothing about. Her sister's entire universe rotated around Orchard Valley and their five-hundred-acre apple orchard ten miles outside of town.

"Colby's one of the best cardiovascular surgeons in the state." Norah didn't bother to disguise her irritation. "Don't you realize what you've done?" she demanded. "You've just insulted one of this country's most—"

"I didn't insult him," Valerie insisted, interrupting her sister's tirade. "I made sure of that myself. Furthermore, you never even let me know he was a heart surgeon— I thought he was just a G.P. And even if he's considered good here in Orchard Valley, Dad needs absolutely the best one available anywhere. Shouldn't you be concerning yourself with his problems and not worrying about offending your doctor boyfriend?"

Norah's eyes widened with shock and hurt. She stood, and without a word walked out of the room, leaving Valerie swamped in immediate remorse. She hadn't meant to snap at her sister, nor had she wanted to sound so overbearing. Referring to Colby as Norah's boyfriend had been childish and petty, which went to prove how badly her nerves were frayed.

The pay phone at the end of the high-ceilinged corridor started to ring and Valerie hurried out of the room, knowing even before she answered that it was Rowdy with the information she'd requested.

"Hello," she said breathlessly, yanking the receiver from the hook.

"Valerie, it's Rowdy. Listen, you're in luck. There's an up-and-coming heart surgeon who's working out of Portland University. Apparently he's developed an innovative surgical technique. I've talked to three of the top heart specialists in the country and they all highly recommend him.''

''Great.'' She groped through her purse until she found a pen and a notebook, which she positioned against the wall. ''Ready.''

''His name is Dr. Colby Winston.''

Valerie dropped her arms and turned to slouch against the wall. ''Dr. Colby Winston,'' she repeated.

''I've got his phone number here.''

''Thanks, Rowdy,'' she said, pride and shame clogging her throat, ''but I've already got it.''

She hadn't been home for twenty-four hours and she'd already managed to alienate her sister, insult a family friend and at the same time disparage a highly regarded doctor.

''Just great, Valerie,'' she muttered to herself. ''Can things get any worse?''

CHAPTER THREE

"STEFFIE?" David Bloomfield's eyes fluttered open and he gazed up at Valerie.

"She'll be here as soon as she can," Valerie reassured him.

How weak he sounded, she thought, as though death was only hours away. Her heart clamored with dread and fear; she wanted to shout at him to fight, to hang on...

That was impossible, and Valerie knew it. In the past two days she'd learned more about the functions of the heart than she'd ever imagined. In more ways than one. She'd learned that the symbolic heart, the center of human emotion, grew larger with the sorrows as well as the joys of love. And the physical heart was subject to its own stresses and risks.

Colby had strived to make the explanation as uncomplicated as possible. Simply put, her father was experiencing heart failure; his heart was pumping blood less efficiently than it should. The decreased strength of the muscles then resulted in distended blood vessels that leaked fluid into his lungs, which interfered with his breathing. Each hour he was growing weaker and closer to death.

"Can't...hold out much longer."

"Of course you can," Valerie insisted, fighting down defeat and discouragement. "You're going to live long enough to be a problem to your children. Isn't that what you've always said? You've got years and years left. Good years, with a houseful of grand-children."

Her father's smile was fleeting at best. "Go home, sweetheart," he whispered. "You haven't even been to the house yet."

"There's nothing there for me without you." She rubbed her thumb soothingly across the back of his hand, avoiding the I.V. needle. "Get well, Daddy, please get well. We all need you."

His eyes drifted shut, and the oppressive need to give in to the weakness of tears nearly overcame her. She blinked furiously in an effort not to cry, succeed-ing despite the enormous lump in her throat.

Valerie was grateful her features were outwardly composed when Colby entered the cubicle a few mo-ments later. He read over the clipboard that outlined her father's progress, then made a brief notation.

"He'll sleep now," he said, guiding her out of the room.

"What's happening?" she asked once they'd left the Coronary Care Unit. "Why is he so much weaker than before? It's like watching his life ebb away. Surely you can do something?" She heard the note of hysteria in her own voice and didn't care. Perhaps she was being selfish for wanting him to live when he so clearly wanted to be released from his life. But she loved him so desperately. She *needed* him, and so did Steffie and Norah.

"We're doing everything we can," Colby assured her.

"I know—but it's not enough."

"Valerie, trust me, I love that crotchety old man myself. I don't want to lose him, either." He led the way to the elevator. "Come on, I'll buy you a cup of coffee."

She was on the verge of pointing out that there was coffee in the waiting room, then hesitated. He was right. She needed a break, even if it was only ten minutes in the hospital cafeteria.

They rode the elevator down to the basement and walked into the large, open room, which was mostly empty now. Colby reached for a serving tray and slid it along the counter, collecting a green dinner salad, a cellophane-wrapped turkey sandwich and coffee. Valerie surveyed the cottage cheese salad with the limp pineapple and instead grabbed a bottle of cranberry juice. She wasn't the least bit hungry, although she'd eaten very little in the past few days.

He withdrew his wallet and paid the cashier, then carried the tray to a table at the back of the room, near the window.

He chose one far removed from any of the occupied tables, and that started Valerie's heart pounding with a renewed sense of anxiety. Colby had brought her here to help her face the inevitable.

"I'm going to lose my father, aren't I?" she asked outright, determined to confront the truth head-on.

Colby looked up, his dark eyes filled with surprise. "Not if I can help it. What makes you ask?"

She slumped against the back of the chair, so relieved that it was all she could do not to weep openly. "I thought that was why you brought me here—what you intended to tell me." With trembling hands, she reached for the container of juice and removed the top.

"We aren't going to lose him." He spoke with such fierce conviction that she realized his will to keep her father alive was as strong as her own.

"How long have you known my father?" she asked, leaning forward and resting her elbows on the table.

"A few years now."

Valerie vaguely recalled hearing Colby's name mentioned once or twice, but she couldn't remember when or for what reason. With her hectic work schedule she'd been home only intermittently. Her last visit had been nearly six months ago, although she phoned weekly.

"We met soon after your mother died," Colby explained. "Your father made a generous donation to the hospital in her name."

Valerie knew that David's contribution had been large enough for the hospital to begin construction of a new wing. The irony of the situation struck her for the first time, and she drew in a deep, painful breath. The new wing housed the Coronary Care Unit.

"Your father and I've played chess once a week or so since then."

"You ever beat him?"

Colby grinned. "Occasionally, but not often."

Valerie was good at chess herself, which was hardly surprising since her father had taught her to play. One day, perhaps, when all this was over, she'd challenge Colby to a game. Odd how easy it was to assume they'd continue to know each other....

"He's very proud of you," Colby stated casually as he unwrapped his sandwich.

Valerie suppressed a sudden urge to giggle. "So—he mentioned me *before* his attack."

"At every opportunity." He frowned as he said it. He was, no doubt, thoroughly sick of the subject.

Valerie settled back and crossed her arms, enjoying herself. "In other words, Dad's preoccupation with matching the two of us up isn't something new."

Colby paused, averting his gaze. "Let's put it this way. He wasn't quite as blatant about it as he's been the past few days."

"You must have been curious about me."

He shrugged. "A bit."

"And?" she prompted. "What do you think?"

Once again Colby lifted his shoulders, as if to say she hadn't impressed him. Or was he saying she hadn't disappointed him? Valerie couldn't tell.

"That doesn't tell me a thing," she complained.

"You're everything your father said and more," he muttered, obviously hoping to satisfy her and at the same time put an end to the conversation.

Valerie knew it was sheer vanity to be so pleased. He might have intended his remark as a compliment, but she didn't read any admiration in his eyes. If Dr. Colby Winston was attracted to her, he concealed it well. She hated to admit how much that dented her pride. The truth was, she wanted him to be fascinated with her. She wanted him to feel enthralled, enchanted, impressed—the way she was with him. Because, despite herself, and despite their awkward beginning, and despite the prospect of a relationship with Rowdy Cassidy, she couldn't get Colby out of her mind.

In a strictly objective way, Valerie knew she was slim and attractive. No matter what her father said about her hair, it was styled in an exuberant tangle of russet curls that highlighted her cheekbones and unusual gray-green eyes.

Those eyes were her greatest asset in the looks department, although her mouth tended to be expressive. Being tall, almost five eight, was a plus, too. Norah was barely five three, and it seemed the entire world towered above her sister. When Valerie wore heels, there wasn't a man in her field she couldn't meet at eye level, which she considered a definite advantage.

"You don't like me, do you?" she asked bluntly.

Her question clearly took him aback, and he hesitated, frowning. "I don't dislike you."

"I make you nervous?"

"Not exactly."

"Then what is it?" she prodded. "Don't worry. I'm not planning to fall in love with you. As I said before, there's someone else on the horizon. I'm just... curious."

"About what?"

"How you feel about me."

His mouth tightened, and Valerie could tell he wasn't accustomed to dealing with a woman as direct as she was. Most men weren't. Valerie didn't believe in suggestion or subtlety. The shortest distance between any two points was a straight line. She'd learned that in high-school geometry and it had worked equally well in life.

"I think you're very good at what you do."

He was sidestepping her question and doing a relatively good job of it, but she wasn't fooled. "Which is?" she pressed.

"Functioning in a male-dominated field."

"Are you implying I've sacrificed my femininity?"

His lips tightened again. "You're good at putting words in someone's mouth, too, aren't you?"

"Sometimes," she agreed, "but only when it suits my purposes."

"No doubt."

"You're not sure how you feel about me, are you?"

"On the contrary, I knew the minute we met."

She cocked an eyebrow, waiting for him to finish. "Well?" she asked when he didn't immediately supply the answer.

"You're bright and attractive."

"Thank you." It wasn't exactly what she'd hoped to hear. He'd revealed no emotion toward her. She'd rarely met a man who was so...she searched for the right word. Staid, she decided. Stoical. He seemed to close himself up whenever he was around her, almost as though he felt he needed protection.

Valerie knew she could be overpowering and opinionated, but she wasn't cold or hard. Just straightforward. They were alike in that way, both sensible, seasoned professionals. It was common ground between them, yet Colby seemed determined to ignore their similarities.

He'd been kind to her, she reminded herself. But she sensed he would have behaved in the same compassionate manner regardless of who she was. Valerie understood that, even applauded it.

So why was she looking for something that wasn't there?

She shook herself mentally. "All right, Dr. Winston," she began in a brisk voice. "Tell me about my father."

NORAH WAS ASLEEP on the sofa when Valerie returned from the cafeteria. She spread the blanket over her sister, wondering why Norah wasn't spending the night at home. Norah stirred, her eyes fluttering open.

"Hello, Sleeping Beauty," Valerie said, smiling softly.

"Where were you?" Norah asked, sitting up. She brushed the hair from her face, and Valerie saw that her soft blue eyes were puffy, as though she'd recently been crying.

"Down in the cafeteria with Colby."

Norah blinked, looking mildly surprised.

"He hadn't had dinner yet and asked me along so we could talk."

"I felt bad about what happened this morning," Norah said. "I was upset about Dad and angry with you for going behind Colby's back. But then I realized I should have explained things better—you know, told you about his qualifications." She sighed. "I was angry that you hadn't talked to me first."

"If I had, I might have saved myself a lot of trouble," Valerie agreed. "Don't worry about it, sis—I would've been upset, too."

"If there was ever a time we need to stick together, it's now. We can't allow a quarrel to come between us."

Valerie nodded. Norah looked small and lost, and Valerie crossed the room to sit down beside her, placing a protective arm around her sister's shoulders.

"I wish Steffie was here," Norah murmured.

Valerie did, too, but in some ways perhaps it was best that their sister hadn't arrived yet. Her absence might well be the only thing keeping their father alive.

"What did you and Colby talk about?" Norah asked, pressing her head against Valerie's shoulder.

"Dad, and what's going to happen."

"Does Colby know?"

Valerie shook her head. "No, but it looks like he may not have the option of waiting until Dad's lungs clear before performing open-heart surgery."

"But his chances of survival would be practically nil if Colby went ahead with it now!"

Valerie had felt the same alarm when Colby described the procedure to her. He'd drawn a detailed outline of the procedure on a napkin and answered a multitude of questions. Although the surgery would be risky, it seemed to be the only alternative available to them. Valerie had understood and accepted Colby's reasoning, even though her father's chances were slim. She prayed it wouldn't come to this, but that was looking less promising every hour.

"The likelihood that he'll survive is a whole lot better with the operation than without," Valerie reminded her sister.

"I know but...oh, Val, it's so scary to think of what our lives would be like without Dad."

"I know." Gently she stroked her sister's hair, offering what reassurance and comfort she could.

"Isn't Colby wonderful?" Norah asked after a while.

Valerie smiled to herself, then nodded. He'd made the surgery, with all its risk, seem the logical thing to do. For the first time since her arrival, she felt hopeful for her father's chances. She held on to that small surge of confidence with both hands. Colby had been patient, answering her questions, giving her reassurance and hope when she'd felt none.

"Now can you understand why everyone likes him so much?" Norah asked, her voice soft.

"Yes." She'd intentionally baited him, determined to find out how he really felt about *her*. She'd looked for some reaction, some sign, but he'd given nothing away.

The more reserved he was, the more challenged she felt. Valerie doubted he'd ever raised his voice or lost his cool, composed air. Even when she'd pressured him, he'd revealed almost no emotion. Yet Valerie couldn't shake the conviction that he was a man of deep feeling—and strong passion.

COLBY WAS SMILING; he'd been smiling ever since he'd left the hospital. He wasn't sure what had prompted him to invite Valerie down to the cafeteria. But he suspected it was because ... well, because he enjoyed being with her. He'd never known a woman who was so willing to speak her feelings. She was direct and honest and, damn it all, *interesting*. It wasn't that he found Sherry, or for that matter Norah, boring. He enjoyed their company in an entirely different way.

But Valerie kept him on his toes. She didn't take anything at face value, but challenged and confronted until she was satisfied. He admired that. In fact, he admired *her*. But that wasn't the end of it. This was a woman he could grow to love.

He'd gone off the deep end. Worked too many hours without a real break. He'd listened to David Bloomfield once too often. There could never be anything between him and Valerie. She wasn't what he needed in a woman; not only that, she'd never be satisfied with life in Orchard Valley again.

And they both knew it.

THE FOLLOWING MORNING, with Norah at the hospital, Valerie felt comfortable about leaving for the first time since her arrival from New York. She desperately needed a change of clothes. She was still wearing the business suit she'd had on when she'd received Norah's message two—no, three—days earlier.

She drove to the family home, down the mile-long driveway that led to the colonial house. She took a moment to glance at the hundreds of neat rows of apple trees, all in fragrant blossom. Then she hauled her suitcase up to her old bedroom, showered and changed into a pair of slacks and a soft blue sweater.

By the time Valerie returned to the hospital she felt a thousand times better. Norah was still asleep, curled up on the sofa, her knees tucked under her chin. She was so blond and delicate that for a moment Valerie had an almost overpowering recollection of their mother. She came to an abrupt stop. The words of greeting froze on her lips and she turned into the hallway.

Quietly she fought back the tears. She'd barely managed to compose herself before Colby strolled purposely down the wide corridor, heading straight toward her, his face taut.

"Have you got a few moments?" he asked stiffly.

"Sure," Valerie said, puzzled by his obvious tension. "Is something wrong? Is it Dad?"

"No, this is between you and me." Colby actually seemed angry. Furious, even, although he hadn't raised his voice. This was certainly the most emotion she'd seen in him yet.

He marched toward the elevator, with Valerie following, and then down the narrow passageway to the back entrance of the hospital and the employee parking lot. He was several yards ahead of her.

"Where are we going?" she demanded. His pace was too swift for her to keep stride with him.

"Outside."

"In case you hadn't noticed, we already are."

"I don't want anyone to hear this."

"Hear *what?*" she almost shrieked, losing her patience.

Colby whirled around to confront her. "I want to know exactly what you said to your father."

Valerie was confused. "About what?"

"Us." The simple little word resonated with anger, contempt, disgust.

Well, so much for her assumption that Colby Winston felt any attraction for her, Valerie mused.

"Us?" she repeated. "Don't be ridiculous. There isn't any us."

"My point exactly," he snapped. "Perhaps you can tell me why your father suddenly announced that you were falling in love with me—and that he expected me to *do* something about it."

"He what?" she exploded.

"You heard me. What in the name of heaven did you say?"

"Nothing." In the three or four times she'd seen him yesterday evening and this morning, her father had been asleep. At least, his eyes had been closed and his breathing was shallow but regular.

"He knew we'd talked in the cafeteria," Colby informed her coolly.

"He did?"

"He mentioned it himself."

"Maybe Norah—"

"Norah nothing. It came straight from the horse's mouth. That and a whole lot more."

Valerie frowned, staring down at the ground in an effort to think.

"Valerie!"

"I...thought he was asleep."

"What did you say?" he demanded a second time.

She was flustered now, which happened so rarely that it unnerved her even more. "Uh...just that we'd talked the other night and I..."

"Go on," he insisted, his jaw muscles tightening.

"I, uh, have this tendency to talk when I'm upset. I don't mind telling you Dad's condition has really scared me. So if he's asleep, like he's been most of today, I sit at his side and tell him the things I've been thinking about."

"Which included me?"

Reluctantly, she nodded. Rarely could she recall being more embarrassed. Color burned in her cheeks.

"Valerie, what did you say to him?" Colby's voice was quiet but his face had sharpened with tension.

Momentarily she closed her eyes. She didn't remember everything she'd mumbled, but what she did recall made her cringe. She'd rambled on, saying whatever came into her mind, and most of her thoughts seemed to concern Colby. Not for a second had she believed her father was awake enough to understand a word of it.

"I told him how impressed I was with you," she began hesitantly. "Although I don't know you well, I sense a strength in you. I told him how grateful I was to you because I've felt so helpless the last couple of days."

She chanced a look in his direction but his expression was impassive. Not knowing what else to do, she continued. "In any family crisis there's always one person who has to be strong, and everyone else leans on that person for support. I'm the oldest and I feel responsible for the others. But when I saw my father that first time, I just couldn't cope. It's even harder for Norah. I realized that the strong one in this situation is you. I told Dad that . . . and some other things.''

"What other things?"

It didn't get any better. "That I . . . found myself attracted to you. Not physically," she rushed to explain, conscious that she was lying. "I'm attracted to the emotional stability I sense in you. Only I didn't bother to explain all that to Dad because I didn't think he could hear me anyway.

"Was that so terrible?" she asked, when Colby remained silent.

"No," he finally admitted in a hoarse voice.

"What exactly did Dad say to you?" she asked curiously.

Colby's gaze touched hers, then withdrew. "That you'd fallen head over heels in love with me. And that's a quote."

"What?" Valerie said incredulously. "No wonder you were so upset."

"Upset's not the word for it. I'm worried about how this is going to affect David's recovery, especially since he seems to have all kinds of expectations now—expectations that are going to be disappointed. I didn't know what you'd told him, but he's built hopes on it. Eventually he'll just have to realize that you're not the kind of woman I intend to marry."

"Believe me, Dr. Winston, you have nothing to worry about," she murmured, annoyed now. "If I *was* going to fall in love, it would be with a man who was a little more sensitive to my pride."

"I apologize," he said, shrugging indifferently. "Your father unfortunately read more into your words. I'm afraid you'll have to say something to him."

"Me?"

"You're the one who started this."

"Why can't we just let the whole thing drop? By tomorrow he'll have forgotten I said anything."

Colby shook his head. "That's not likely. He asked me to bring in a preacher so we could be married at his bedside."

Valerie couldn't help it, she burst out laughing. It was as though all the tension, all the waiting and frustration had broken free inside her. She laughed until the tears streaked down her face and her sides ached, and even then she couldn't stop. Clutching her stomach, she wiped the moisture from her cheeks.

"Colby, darling," she said between giggles. "What shall I wear to the ceremony?"

Colby apparently didn't find her antics at all humorous.

"I'll want children, of course," she told him when she'd managed to stop giggling. "Nine or ten, and I'll name the little darlings after you. There'll be little cheeses running around our happy home—Cheddar and—"

"I have absolutely no intention of marrying you."

"Of course you don't right *now,* but that'll all change." She found that she enjoyed teasing him, and the laughter was a welcome release after all the tension of the past few days.

"You're not serious, are you?"

Valerie sighed deeply. "If you want me to say something to Dad, I will."

"I think that would be best."

"I'm really not so bad, you know," she felt obliged to tell him. She was disappointed in his reaction, although she'd never admit it. If she was going to make a fool of herself over a man she didn't need to travel across the country to do so!

"We don't have a thing in common and shouldn't pretend we do."

"Well, but—"

"Let's leave it at that, Valerie."

His attitude hurt. "Fine. I'm not interested in you, either," she muttered. Without another word, she turned around and marched back into the hospital.

The man had his nerve. He made a relationship with her sound about as attractive as one with a . . . a porcupine! Colby acted as though she'd purposely set a trap for him, and she resented that.

Norah was awake when she returned to the waiting room. Her younger sister looked up, smiling, as Valerie hurried in and began to pace.

"Is something wrong?" Norah asked, pouring herself a cup of coffee. She gestured toward the pot, but Valerie shook her head.

"Have you ever noticed how opinionated and high-handed Colby Winston can be?" she asked, still pacing furiously.

"Dr. Winston?" Norah repeated, amazed. "Not in the least. I've never known him to be rude, not even when someone deserved it."

Valerie impatiently pushed the sleeves of her sweater past her elbows. "I don't think I've ever known a man who irritated me more."

"I thought you liked him."

"I thought I did, too," she answered darkly.

"Steffie phoned," Norah said, cutting off Valerie's irritation as effectively as if she'd flipped a light switch. "She got through to the nurses' station here when she couldn't reach either of us at the house."

"Where is she?" Valerie asked. "Is the transportation strike over?"

"No," Norah said with a shrug. "She's still trapped in whatever the name of that town is. If she was in one of the big cities I don't think she'd be having nearly as much trouble. She asked about Dad, and I told her that everything's about the same. She sounded so worried . . . I think she was close to tears."

"Poor Steffie."

"She said she'd give everything she owns to find a way home." Norah shook her head. "If something doesn't break soon, I think Steff's going to hike her way over the Alps."

She'd do it, too; Valerie didn't doubt that for a moment.

"I was with Dad earlier," Norah said, changing the subject a second time. "He was a little more alert than he has been."

Valerie frowned, well aware of the reason. Her dear, manipulative father seemed to think he was about to get his wish. Little did he realize she had no intention of marrying Dr. Colby Winston. Or that Colby was no more interested in her than she was in him.

CHAPTER FOUR

DAVID BLOOMFIELD'S condition didn't change throughout the day that followed. Valerie saw Colby intermittently. He was in surgery most of the afternoon and stopped in, still wearing his surgical gown, to check on her father early that evening. Valerie happened to be there at the time, and she read the weariness in Colby's face. Without saying anything to her father, she followed Colby out of the room.

"How about a cup of coffee?" she suggested, and when he hesitated, she added lightly, "I thought you might like to know how I warded off the preacher."

He grinned, then rubbed a hand across his eyes. "All right," he said, checking his watch. "Give me fifteen minutes and I'll meet you in the cafeteria."

Valerie headed downstairs, taking her briefcase with her. Early that afternoon she'd had her secretary fax the contents of several files to her. Even if she had to be out of the office while her father was ill, there were still matters that required her attention. She'd spent the better part of the afternoon calling clients and updating her files. Working out of the hospital waiting room wasn't ideal, but she'd managed.

She was reading over her notes when Colby arrived. As he pulled out a chair, she straightened, tucked the papers inside her briefcase and closed it.

After a somewhat perfunctory greeting, Colby reached for the sugar canister in the middle of the table and methodically poured out a teaspoon, briskly stirring it into the hot coffee. "I wanted to apologize," he began.

His words took her by surprise. "For what?"

"I was out of line, coming down on you the way I did about the marriage business. I should have realized your father was stretching whatever you said out of proportion. I took my irritation out on you."

She dismissed his apology with a shake of her head. "It was understandable—don't worry about it. As far as I'm concerned, the entire matter's forgotten."

His eyes met hers as though he couldn't quite believe her. "You spoke to him?" he asked abruptly.

Valerie nodded, trying to disguise her amusement. "My poor father was devastated, or at least he tried to persuade me he was. But—" she sighed expressively "—he'll get over it just as I will." She fluttered her eyelashes melodramatically, teasing Colby just a little.

His eyes shot to hers, and a slow grin moved across his face, relaxing his features. "Disappointed, were you?"

"Oh, yes. I've always dreamed of a traditional white wedding gown—one that matches the sheets on my father's hospital bed." She smiled and relaxed, too, feeling at ease with him now. She'd been angry, but that was over, and she had to admit she actually liked this man. She certainly admired him.

Colby sipped his coffee, and once again she noted the lines of fatigue that marked his eyes and mouth.

"Rough day?"

He nodded. "I lost a patient. Mrs. Murphy. She died this afternoon in surgery. We knew there was a risk, but..." He shrugged heavily. "No matter how often it happens, I never get used to it."

"I'm so sorry, Colby." Her hand reached for his in a gesture of friendship and understanding.

His fingers gripped hers as if to absorb the comfort and consolation she offered. At the feel of his hand closing over hers, Valerie felt a thrill of happiness, and even more inexplicable, a sense of *rightness*. She didn't know how else to describe it. Yet almost immediately, the doubts and uncertainties flowed into her mind.

They were friends, nothing more, she reminded herself. Neither of them was looking for anything else. Neither of them *wanted* anything else. But if that was really the case, why should she experience this deep ache of longing? For one impulsive moment she yearned to burrow her way into his arms, rest her head against his shoulder and immerse herself in his strength. Lend him hers.

Valerie decided she had to ignore these uncharacteristic sensations. She withdrew her hand, hoping he wouldn't notice the telltale tremble.

"I'd better get back before Norah wonders where I am," she said firmly. Valerie was a woman who needed to be in control, who looked at a problem from all angles and worked toward the most favorable solution. But Colby Winston wasn't a problem that needed to be solved. He was a man who left her feeling vulnerable and confused.

She was already on her feet, briefcase in hand, when Colby spoke. "Don't go...not yet." His voice was soft, hesitant.

Unsure, Valerie sank back into her chair, helpless to refuse him.

"No, never mind." Colby shook his head, eyes suddenly guarded. "Actually, I should be leaving myself," he said quickly, bounding to his feet. He drank down several gulps of coffee, then strode out of the cafeteria, with Valerie following close behind.

"Colby." She stopped him in front of the elevator. "What is it you don't like about me?" The question was out before she had time to analyze the wisdom of asking.

"I do like you," he answered, frowning.

"But you wouldn't want to marry someone like me?"

"No," he agreed calmly. "I wouldn't want to marry someone like you."

"Because?" Valerie wasn't sure why she continued to probe, why it was necessary for her to understand his reasons. She only knew that she felt a compelling urge to ask.

"You have a brilliant future ahead of you," he said, not meeting her eyes. "Your father's proud of your accomplishments, and rightly so. I admire your drive, your ambition, your ability."

"But." She said it before he could. There had to be a *but* in there somewhere.

"But," he said with the slightest hint of a smile. "I'm not interested in becoming involved with an up-and-coming female executive. When it comes to committing myself to a woman and a relationship, I want someone who's more...traditional. Someone who'll consider making our home and rearing our children her career."

"I see." He was wise to recognize that she wasn't the type who'd be content to sit quietly by the fireplace and spin her own yarn. No, Valerie would soon figure out how to have that yarn mass-produced, then see about franchising it into a profit-making enterprise. Business was in her blood, the same way medicine was in his.

"I don't mean to offend you," he said.

"You haven't," she assured him, and it was the truth.

The elevator arrived and they stepped inside together. Neither spoke as Colby pushed the appropriate button. The doors silently glided shut.

Valerie wished they weren't alone. It seemed so intimate, so private, just the two of them standing there.

"Valerie, listen..."

"It's all right," she said, smiling up at him. "Really. I asked, didn't I? That's the way I am. You were honest with me, and I appreciate that. It's true I'm attracted to you, but that's probably fairly common in our circumstances. Being attracted doesn't mean I'm in love with you."

"I know, it's just that—" He broke off hastily, his eyes probing hers. "Oh, what the hell," he murmured, the words so low that Valerie had to strain to hear him. Then his hands were taking hold of her shoulders and drawing her toward him. His mouth unerringly found hers and without conscious intent, she responded to his kiss, feeling none of the awkwardness she experienced with other men. Delicious tremors were moving down her spine. The kiss was much like the man. Gentle, deliberate, devastating.

She heard a soft moan easing its way from the back of her throat.

His head shifted restlessly before he released her. He dropped his arms, looking completely shocked. Valerie didn't know what had distressed him most—the fact that he'd kissed her or that he'd enjoyed it.

"Valerie, I . . ." Her name was a whisper.

Just then the elevator doors opened, and Colby cast an accusing glare at the nurse who entered. Grabbing Valerie's hand, he jerked her onto the floor before the elevator doors closed again.

"This isn't CCU," she protested, glancing around. Good grief, they were on the maternity floor. Directly down the hall, a row of newborns was on display behind a glass partition.

But Colby didn't give her a chance to get a closer look. Still holding her hand, he led her to the stairwell. He held open the door for her, then dashed up the steps. He was halfway up the first flight before he seemed to realize she was no longer beside him. He turned back impatiently.

"Colby," she objected. "If you want to run up the stairs, fine, but you're in better physical condition than I am. I sit at a desk most of the day, remember?"

"I didn't mean for that to happen."

"What, racing up the stairs?"

"No, kissing you!"

"It was nice enough, as kisses go," she said, out of breath from the exertion, "but don't worry, you aren't going to have to marry me because of a simple kiss." The only way she could deal with this experience was to deny how strongly it affected her, push aside these unfamiliar, unwelcome feelings. She suspected that was how Colby felt, too.

"Our kiss may have been a lot of things, but simple wasn't one of them," he muttered.

"You're worrying too much about something that really isn't important."

His eyes held such a quizzical expression that Valerie continued talking. "You're tired, and so am I," she said, making excuses for them both. "We're under a lot of stress. You've had a long, discouraging day and your guard slipped a little," she went on. "My being so damn pushy didn't help matters, either. You kissed me, but it isn't the end of the world."

"It won't happen again." He spoke with absolute certainty.

Pride stiffened Valerie's shoulders. "That's probably for the best." Colby was right. Her personality was all wrong for someone like him. A doctor's work was emotionally and physically draining; she couldn't blame him for seeking a wife who'd create a warm cocoon of domesticity for him. A home filled with comfort and love and peace. Valerie couldn't fault his preference. She wished him well and determined to put the kiss out of her mind, once and for all.

THE STREETS of downtown Orchard Valley greeted Valerie like a long-lost friend. Her heart cheered at the sight of the bright, flower-filled baskets that hung from every streetlight.

The clock outside the Wells Fargo Bank was still ten minutes slow, even after thirty years. When Valerie was thirteen, a watchsmith from somewhere out East had arrived to repair the grand old clock. He spent the better part of a day working on it, then declared the problem solved. Two days after he'd left town, the clock was back to running ten minutes late and no one bothered to have it repaired again, although it came up on the town council agenda at least once a year.

The barber shop with its red-and-white striped pole whirling round and round like a fat candy cane was as cheery as ever. Mr. Stein, the barber, sat in one of his leather chairs reading the *Orchard Valley Clarion,* waiting for his next customer. Valerie walked past, and when he glanced over the top of the paper, she smiled and waved. He grinned and returned the gesture.

The sense of homecoming was strong, lifting her spirits. She strolled past the newspaper office, two doors down from the barber shop; looking in the window, she noted the activity inside as the staff prepared the next edition of the *Orchard Valley Clarion.* She hadn't gone more than a few steps when she heard someone call her name.

She turned to find Charles Tomaselli, the paper's editor, directly behind her. "Valerie, hello. I wondered how long it'd take before I ran into you. How's your dad doing?"

"About the same," she answered.

"I'm sorry to hear that." He buried his hands in his pants pockets and matched his pace to hers. "I haven't seen Stephanie around."

"She's still in Italy."

Although he gave no outward indication of his feelings, Valerie sensed his irritation. "She didn't bother to come home even when her father's so ill? I'd have thought she'd want to be with him."

"She's trying as hard as she can," Valerie said, defending her sister. "But she's stuck in a small town a hundred or so miles outside of Rome—because of that transportation strike. But if there's a way out, Steffie'll find it."

Charles nodded, and Valerie had the odd impression that he regretted bringing up the subject of her sister. "If you get the chance, will you tell your father something for me?"

"Of course."

"Let him know Commissioner O'Dell called me following last week's article on the farm labor issue. That'll cheer him up."

"The farm labor issue?" Valerie repeated, wanting to be sure she understood him correctly.

Charles grinned almost boyishly, his dark eyes sparkling with pleasure. "That's right. I don't know if you're aware of this, but your father would make one hell of an investigative reporter. Tell him I said that, too. He'll know what I mean."

"All right," Valerie agreed, wishing she knew more about the article and her father's role in it.

"Nice seeing you again," Charles said, turning to head back to the newspaper office. He hesitated.

"When you see Stephanie, tell her I said hello, will you?"

"Of course. I'll be happy to." Thoughtfully, Valerie watched him walk away from her. Charles not only edited the *Clarion*, he wrote a regular column and most of the major features, like the farm labor story he'd just mentioned. Considering his talent and energy, she was surprised that he'd stayed on with a small-town paper; he could have gone to work for one of the big dailies long before now.

She found it interesting that he'd asked about Steffie. Several years ago, Valerie had felt sure there was something romantic developing between them. Steffie had been a college student at the time and Charles had recently moved to Orchard Valley. She remembered Steffie poring over every article, every column, exclaiming over Charles's skill, his style, his wit. To Valerie, it had sounded like romance in the making.

But then, romance was hardly a subject she knew much about. So if there was something between Steffie and Charles, it was their business and she was staying out of it. She knew just enough about relationships to make a real mess of them. A good example of that was how she'd bungled things with Colby.

She experienced a twinge of regret. Since their kiss, he'd been avoiding her. Or at least she assumed he was. Until then, he'd made a point of stopping in and chatting with her when he could. They'd always been brief visits, but their times together had broken up the monotony of the long hours she'd spent at the hospital. She hadn't realized how much those short interludes meant to her until they stopped.

Norah was the one who'd sent Valerie on the errand into town. Some flimsy excuse about picking up a roll of film their father had left for developing. It was a blatant attempt to get her out of the hospital— not that Valerie minded. She was beginning to feel desperate for clean, fresh air and sunshine.

Although most of the orchards were miles out of town, she could have sworn that when she inhaled deeply she caught a whiff of the apple blossoms, which were just beginning to bud.

Spring had always been her favorite time of year. But although she'd been home intermittently over the years, she'd never spent more than a day or two and had never visited during April or May. She wondered now if she'd been unconsciously avoiding Orchard Valley then, knowing the charm and the appeal of her home would be at their strongest during those two months. Perhaps she'd feared she might never want to leave if she came while the white and pink blossoms perfumed the air.

Not wanting to examine her thoughts too closely, Valerie continued down the street, past the feed store and the local café until she arrived at her destination. Al's Pharmacy.

Al's was a typical small-town drugstore, where you could buy anything from cards and gifts to aspirin and strawberry jam. At one end of the pharmacy Al operated a state-run liquor store and in the opposite corner was a small post office. The soda fountain, which specialized in chocolate malts, was situated at the front. Valerie had lost count of the number of times she'd stopped in after school with her friends. She wondered if "going to Al's for a chocolate malt" remained as popular with teenagers these days as it had been when she was growing up. She suspected it did.

"Valerie Bloomfield," the aging pharmacist called to her from behind the counter. "I thought that was you. How's your dad doing?"

"The same."

"Norah phoned and said you were on your way. I put those snapshots aside for you and just wrote it up on the bill. You tell your dad I'm counting on him to go fishing with me come July, and I won't take no for an answer this year."

"I'll tell him," Valerie promised.

She collected the package and wandered outside. Curiosity got the better of her, though, and she paused on the sidewalk to open the envelope. Inside was an array of snapshots her father had taken earlier in the month.

Valerie's heart constricted at the number of photos he had of her mother's grave site. In each, a profusion of flowers adorned the headstone. There were a couple of shots of Norah, as well. The first showed her sitting in the chair by the fireplace, a plaid blanket tucked around her knees and an open book on her lap. The second picture was taken outside, probably in late March. The wind had whipped Norah's blond hair about her face, and she was laughing into the sun. In both photographs her resemblance to their mother was uncanny.

Grief and pity tugged at Valerie's heart as she imagined her father snapping those pictures. He was so lost and lonely without his Grace, and the photographs told her that in an unmistakable and poignant way.

Her thoughts oppressive, Valerie walked aimlessly for some minutes. When she saw that she was near the community park, she strolled in, past the swimming pool, now drained and empty, and followed the stone walkway that meandered through the manicured lawns. As she reached the children's playground, a gentle breeze caught the swings, rocking them back and forth.

Memories of her childhood flooded her mind, and she sat in one of the old swings, almost wishing she were a little girl again. It would have been easy to close her eyes, pretending she was eight years old. She allowed herself a minute to remember Sunday afternoons spent in this very park, with David pushing her and a tiny Stephanie on these swings, catching them at the bottom of the slide. But she was twenty-eight now and her father, whom she adored, was fighting for each breath he drew in a hospital room.

She refused to even consider the thought of losing him. Was she being selfish and thoughtless? Valerie wondered. She didn't know. Her father was ready to die, ready to relinquish his life.

She dragged the toe of her shoe along the ground, slowing the swing to a halt. When the time came to let go of her father, Valerie prayed it would be with acceptance and strength. When death came to him, she wanted it to be as a friend, not an enemy with a score to settle. *But not yet. Please, not yet.*

As she drove back toward the hospital, past the strip malls that marked the highway, she caught sight of a recent addition. A movie theater, a six-plex. It astonished her that little Orchard Valley would have six movies all playing at once. The downtown theater she remembered so well from her teenage years still operated, but to a limited audience; according to Norah the features were second-run and often second-rate.

Orchard Valley had its share of national fast-food restaurants now, too, many of them situated along the highway. But as far as Valerie was concerned, hamburgers didn't get any better than those at The Burger Shack, a locally owned drive-in.

The summer she was sixteen, Valerie had worked there as a car hop, waiting on customers for minimum wage, thinking she was the luckiest girl in town to have landed such a wonderful job. How times had changed! How much *she'd* changed.

As she neared the hospital, Valerie felt a reluctance take hold of her heart. For nearly a week now, she'd virtually lived on the CCU floor with only brief visits home to shower and change clothes. It had been a strange week, outside ordinary time somehow. Nearly four years ago, when her mother was dying, she'd experienced something similar. But then her father and both her sisters had been there to share it. Now there were only two—she and Norah. And Colby...

She pulled into the parking lot and found a vacant spot, then walked toward the main entrance, sorry to leave the sunshine.

The minute she entered the lobby, Norah sprang up from the sofa she'd been sitting on. "I didn't think you'd ever get back," she said breathlessly. "What took you so long?"

"I stopped off at the park. What's the matter?"

"Steffie called from Rome. She's flying home by way of Tokyo. I know it sounds crazy, but it was the most direct flight she could catch. She's hoping to arrive sometime tomorrow night. She wasn't sure exactly when, but she said she'd let us know as soon as possible."

"How'd she make it to Rome?"

"I asked her the same thing, but she didn't have time to explain. I told Dad she'd probably be here by tomorrow night."

Valerie felt herself relax. Until now, she hadn't realized just how tense she'd been over Steffie's situation.

"Colby wants to see you," Norah informed her next.

"Did he say why?"

Norah shook her head, frowning a little. "You two didn't have an argument, did you?"

"No. What makes you ask?"

Norah shrugged vaguely. "Just the way he looked when he asked for you."

"Looked?"

"Oh, I don't know," Norah said, clearly regretting that she'd said anything. "It was like he was eager to see you, but then relieved when I told him you'd gone into town. I know that sounds absurd, but I can't think of any better way of describing it."

"I'll catch him later." For some reason, Valerie wasn't quite ready to see him yet.

"I'm sure he'll stop by this evening."

"How's Dad doing?" Valerie asked as they headed for the elevator.

"Not so good. His breathing is more labored and the swelling in his extremities isn't any better. That's not a good sign. Colby's doing everything he can to drain his lungs, but nothing seems to work. In the meantime, Dad's growing weaker every hour."

"He misses Mom even more than we realized," Valerie whispered, thinking about the snapshots she'd picked up at Al's Pharmacy. She wondered how often he'd visited their mother's grave without anyone's knowing. How often he turned to speak to the woman he'd spent a lifetime with, remembering too late that she was gone.

"What will we do if anything happens to Dad?" Norah asked quietly.

A few days earlier, Valerie would have rejected that possibility, adamantly claiming their father wasn't going to die. She'd stubbornly refused to consider it. She wasn't nearly as unyielding now.

"I don't know," she admitted, "but we'll manage. We'll have to."

They were seated in the waiting room when Colby arrived. Valerie glanced up from a business publication she was reading and knew instantly that something was wrong. Terribly wrong. His eyes, dark and troubled, held hers for several seconds. Without being consciously aware of it, she stood, the magazine slipping unnoticed to the floor.

"Colby?" His name became an urgent plea. "What's happened?"

He sat down on the sofa and reached for Valerie's hands, gripping them tightly with his own. His gaze slid from her to Norah. "Your father's suffered a second heart attack."

"No," Norah breathed.

"And?" Valerie's own heart felt as though it were in danger of failing just then. It pounded wildly, sending bursts of fear through her body.

"We can't delay the surgery any longer."

Norah was on her feet, tears streaking her face. "You can't do the surgery now! His chances of survival are practically nil. We both know that."

"He doesn't have *any* chance if we don't." Although he was speaking to Norah, it was Valerie's gaze he held, Valerie's eyes he looked into—as if to say he'd do anything to have spared her this.

CHAPTER FIVE

COLBY HAD BEEN with her father in the operating room almost six hours, but to Valerie, it felt like six years.

While she waited, she recalled the happy times with her father and, especially as she grew into adolescence, the not-so-happy ones. Her will had clashed often with his, and they'd engaged in one verbal battle after another. Valerie had found her father stubborn, high-handed and irrational.

Her mother had repeatedly assured Valerie the reason she didn't get along with her father was that the two of them were so much alike. At the time Valerie had considered her mother's remark an insult. Furthermore, it made no sense. If they were alike, then they should be friends instead of adversaries.

It wasn't until her mother became ill that Valerie grew close to her father. In their concern and love for Grace, they'd set aside their own differences; not a cross word had passed between them since.

Valerie couldn't say which of them had changed, but she figured they'd both made progress. All she knew was that she loved her father with a fierceness that left her terrified whenever she thought about losing him.

The passage of time lost all meaning as she paced, back and forth, across the waiting room floor. It wasn't the waiting room she was so familiar with, since Surgery was on the hospital's ground level; a small brick patio, bordered with a waist-high hedge, opened off glass doors. Every now and again, Valerie or Norah would wander outside to breathe in the cool night air, to savor the peace and tranquility of the night.

Somehow word got out about her father's crisis. Pastor Wallen from the Community Church stopped by and prayed with Valerie and Norah. Charles Tomaselli was there for an hour, as well. Al Russell from the pharmacy and several other friends came, too.

At midnight, an exhausted Norah had curled up on the sofa and fallen into a troubled sleep. Valerie envied her sister's ability to rest, but found no such respite for her own fears.

Pacing and sucking on hard candy to relieve her nerves were the only methods she had of dealing with the terrible tension. After her third roll of candy, she'd joked to Norah that she had fabulous lungs from not smoking, but her teeth were in danger of rotting from all the sugar.

Now she stood staring out the window at the bright moon-filled night. She turned suddenly when she heard a soft footfall behind her. Colby stood there, still wearing his surgical greens.

Valerie's eyes flew to his, but she could read nothing.

"He made it."

She nearly slumped to the floor with relief. Tears filled her eyes, but she promptly blinked them back.

"Thank God," she whispered, raising both hands to cover her mouth.

"I nearly lost him once," Colby said hoarsely, shaking his head. How exhausted he looked, Valerie noted. "I didn't think there was anything more we could do. It seemed like a miracle when his heart restarted. In some ways, it was. Only so much of what happens on the operating table is in my hands."

"I'm sure it was a miracle," Valerie whispered, hardly able to speak. She walked to the sofa on unsteady legs and bent to wake Norah. Her sister woke instantly—her training as a nurse, no doubt—and Valerie told her, "Dad made it through the operation."

"The danger's not over yet," Colby cautioned. "Not by a long shot. I wish I could tell you otherwise, but I can't. If he survives the night—"

"But he survived the surgery," Norah said, her voice raised with expectant hope. "I didn't think that would be possible. Surely that was his biggest hurdle?"

"Yes," Colby agreed, "but his condition is extremely critical."

"I know," Norah answered, but a faint light began to glow in her eyes. From the little Norah had said, Valerie realized her sister hadn't expected their father to live through the ordeal. Now that he had, she was given the first glimmer of promise.

"I'll be back in a few minutes," Colby said, rubbing his eyes in an oddly vulnerable gesture. He must be running on pure adrenaline, Valerie thought. He'd been in surgery earlier in the day and he'd lost a patient; he'd feared he was about to lose another one. He still could. He didn't need to say it aloud for Valerie to know.

Colby didn't expect her father to live until morning.

"I wish Steffie was here," Norah whispered after Colby had left.

Valerie also yearned for her missing sister. "I do, too."

Colby had been gone only a couple of minutes when a male nurse appeared. He knew Norah and greeted her warmly, then told them they could each see their father, but for only a moment.

Valerie went first. She'd assumed she was emotionally prepared, but the sight of her father destroyed any self-control she might have attained. Seeing him lying there so close to death affected her far more acutely than she'd anticipated.

Hurriedly she turned and left, feeling as though she could barely breathe. She walked past Norah and the others without a word. She stumbled onto the patio, hugging her arms around her middle, dragging in one deep breath after another in a futile effort to compose herself.

The tears, which she'd managed to resist all evening, broke through in a flood of fear and anger. It was *unfair*. It was so unfair. How could she lose her father so soon after her mother?

She didn't often give in to tears, but now they came as a release. Huge sobs shook her shoulders. Slowly, she lowered herself onto a concrete bench, then rocked

back and forth as the hot, unstoppable tears continued to fall.

A hand at her back felt warm and gentle. "Go
ahead and let it out," Colby whispered.

He sat beside her, his arm around her shoulders,
and gradually drew her to him. She had no strength or
will to resist. Nestling her face against his jacket, Valerie sobbed loudly, openly. Colby rubbed his cheek
along her hair and whispered indistinguishable,
soothing words. His arms were strong and safe, and
she desperately needed him and he was there.

When there were no more tears left to shed, a deep
shudder racked her body. She straightened and used
her sleeve to wipe her damp face.

"Feel better?" Colby asked softly, his hand brush-
ing the hair away from her temple.

Valerie nodded, embarrassed now that he'd found
her like this. "Norah?"

"She's talking to Mark Collins. One of the nurses
who assisted me in surgery."

"I...thought I was prepared...didn't know I'd fall
apart like this."

"You've been under a lot of strain."

"We all have." She edged away from him, and taking the cue, he dropped her arm. She offered him a
trembling smile, her gaze avoiding his.

"I'd give anything to be able to assure you your
father's going to make it through this," he said, his
voice heavy. "But I can't do that, Val."

"I know." Spontaneously, as though he'd silently
willed it, she raised her eyes to his. His hands grasped
her shoulders, tightening as he urged her closer. His

eyes seemed to darken as his mouth made a slow descent toward hers, stopping a mere fraction from her lips.

Valerie closed her eyes, and his warm breath caressed her face. She inhaled the pungent scent of surgical soap and something else, something that was ineffably him.

"We shouldn't be doing this," he whispered.

It certainly wasn't what she'd expected him to say. "I...know," she agreed, but she was beyond listening to common sense. She needed Colby. His warmth, his comfort, his touch. And she wouldn't be denied.

"Please," she whispered.

The driving force of his kiss parted her lips, and Valerie was instantly caught in a whirlwind of sensation. Her hands reached for him, sliding up his solid chest, her fingers locking at the base of his neck.

He moaned, and she did, too. There was no resistance in Valerie, none. Willingly she surrendered herself to his kiss, to his need and her own.

With what seemed like reluctance, he broke away and slipped his mouth from hers, burning a path down her neck to the hollow of her throat.

She felt instantly cold when he lifted his face. Opening her eyes, she glanced toward the waiting room, grateful to see that it was empty. They were alone in the shadows of the hedge, but a few seconds earlier it wouldn't have mattered if they'd been standing in the middle of the bustling emergency room.

"I shouldn't have let that happen. We both—"

Valerie placed her finger over his lips, silencing him. "Don't say it. Please." Her hands cupped his face and she gazed into his eyes, dark now with desire. "I need you. Right or wrong, I need you. Just hold me."

A faint quiver went through her as he brought her back into his arms. Closing her eyes again, Valerie surrendered to the strength and safety she felt in the circle of his embrace.

He kissed her forehead lightly. His breath was uneven, and she found pleasure in knowing that he was no less affected by their encounter than she was.

As she'd already told him, Valerie didn't want to question the right or wrong of it now. Neither of them was in any real danger of falling in love. Colby had already explained the reasons a relationship was unfeasible for them. And she agreed with him. But their calm, rational words didn't take into account what she was experiencing now. This excitement, this weightless sense of release and longing. She didn't want it to end. Apparently Colby didn't, either, because he made no move to let her go.

"You shouldn't feel so good in my arms," he told her gently.

"I'm sorry." But she wasn't, not really. Soon they'd both regret these moments, but she'd save all the remorse for another time.

While she was in Colby's embrace, she didn't have to think about what the future might hold. She didn't have to worry about facing the world without anyone to guide and support her. For the first time since she'd come home to Orchard Valley, Valerie didn't feel inadequate or alone.

True, Norah was with her and Steffie was due to arrive any time. The three of them had each other, yet

Valerie couldn't quite escape the old roles; she was the one they'd always depended on for encouragement, guidance, a sense of strength. Only Valerie didn't feel strong. She felt shaken, knocked off balance. She felt completely helpless . . .

"Norah's looking for you," Colby whispered close to her ear.

Valerie sighed and grudgingly broke away from him. She glanced into the waiting room and noticed her younger sister. Norah's gaze found her at the same moment. She didn't do a good job of concealing her surprise.

Valerie stood and turned to Colby. "Thank you."

He remained sitting on the concrete bench and sent her a smile full of private meaning.

Norah met her at the door, her eyes shifting from Valerie to Colby. "Is everything all right?"

Valerie nodded. "Dad's doing as well as we can expect."

"I didn't mean Dad. I meant with you."

"Of course," Valerie answered, forcing a light, casual tone. "I . . . just needed a good cry, and Colby lent me his shoulder."

Norah slipped her arm around Valerie's waist. "His shoulder, you say?" she asked, with more than a hint of a smile in her soft voice. "It looked like more than that to me."

"DAD'S BEEN ASLEEP for nearly twenty hours." Valerie voiced her concern to Norah, who was far more knowledgeable about what was and wasn't usual following this kind of surgery. "Isn't that too long? I realize the anesthesia has a lot to do with it, but I can't help worrying."

"He's been awake for brief periods off and on today," Norah assured her. "He's doing very well, all things considered."

Her father wasn't Valerie's only concern. It was now after nine in the evening, and she'd been waiting since morning for some word from Steffie, who was supposed to be arriving sometime that day. But no one had heard from her, and Valerie couldn't help feeling anxious.

"Dad tried to talk the last time I was with him," Norah told her.

"What did he say?"

She shrugged. "It didn't make any sense. He looked up at me and blinked, then grinned as if he'd heard the funniest joke in years and said 'six kids.'"

"Six kids?"

"I don't get it, either," Norah continued. "I'm going to ask Colby about it when I see him, but we keep missing each other."

Valerie sat down and thumbed through the frayed pages of a two-year-old women's magazine. It was a summer issue dedicated to homes and gardens, which only went to prove how desperate she was for reading material that would take her mind off her fears.

She glanced at photographs of bright glossy kitchens and "country" bedrooms, wicker-furnished porches and "southwest-themed" living rooms—all of them attractive, none of them quite real. None of them *home*.

And she knew with sudden certainty that home was here. Here in Orchard Valley, in the upstairs bedroom at the end of the hallway. Home was curling up with a good book by the fireplace in her father's den, and it was eating meals around the big oak table in the dining room her mother had loved.

That was home. She *lived* in her Texas condo in an executive neighborhood. She'd had a decorator choose the color scheme and select the furniture since she didn't have the time for either task. A housekeeper came in twice a week to clean. The condo was a place to sleep. An address where she could pick up her mail. But it wasn't a place of memories and it wasn't home.

She read an article in the same magazine about herb gardens. Gardening had always been her mother's hobby, but every now and then Valerie had helped her weed. The times they'd shared working in the garden were among the fondest memories she had of her mother.

Perhaps in an attempt to recapture some of that simple happiness, Valerie had bought several large plants. But the housekeeper was the one who watered and fertilized them, since Valerie traveled so much.

Neither a home, at least not like the one she'd been raised in, nor a garden seemed to be in her future. Colby had recognized that from the beginning. Just as well, although it hadn't warded off the magnetic attraction between them.

Valerie's mind wandered to their exchange the night before. Their kissing was undoubtedly a mistake, but it was understandable, and certainly forgivable. Both were emotionally drained, their resistance to each other almost nonexistent. Yet Valerie couldn't bring herself to regret the time she'd spent in Colby's arms.

It hurt a bit that he was avoiding her, because it told her he didn't share her feelings. In those moments with Colby, Valerie had experienced something extraordinary. She'd always considered romantic love a highly overrated commodity. Dr. Colby Winston was the first man who'd given her reason to reevaluate that opinion.

Just when she was beginning to think he planned never to seek her out again, Colby surprised her. Norah had gone to talk with the nurse who'd been assigned to care for their father, and Valerie sat alone in the SICU waiting room, shuffling through her thoughts. Colby was on her mind just then—not that he was ever far from her musings.

She happened to glance up as he walked in. He was wearing a dark gray suit; she didn't think she'd ever seen a handsomer man.

Their eyes met and held. "Hello," she said, with a breathless quality to her voice. Over the course of her career, Valerie had made presentations before large audiences. Her voice was strong and carried well, yet when it came to Colby she felt like a first-grader asked to stand before the class and confess a wrong.

"Valerie." He paused and cleared his throat, then began again, sounding stilted and formal. "I've tied up matters here and I'm addressing a seminar this evening at the university. However, I have time for a bite to eat before I leave. Would you join me?"

"I'd be happy to," she answered automatically.

"I thought we might eat someplace other than the cafeteria." His voice was more relaxed now. "There's an Italian restaurant near here that serves excellent food."

"Great." Valerie brightened until she realized he hadn't chosen the restaurant because he had a craving for spaghetti. He wanted to talk to her somewhere away from the hospital. Somewhere he could be assured none of his peers would be listening.

After leaving word for Norah, they left the hospital in his car, a late-model maroon sedan. Sitting beside him, watching his strong, well-shaped hands on the steering wheel, gave Valerie a sense of intimacy, a feeling of familiarity.

The restaurant was elegantly decorated in black and silver. The lighting, low and discreet, created a welcoming impression.

"You didn't need to pay for my dinner to apologize, you know," Valerie said, reading over her menu. She quickly decided on a bowl of minestrone soup and fettuccine with fresh asparagus. No wine, because it would send her to sleep.

"Apologize?" Colby repeated.

Valerie lowered her menu, and crossing her arms, leaned toward him. "Not apologize exactly. You brought me here to tell me you regret what happened last night, didn't you? I mean, it's fairly obvious, since you've been avoiding me all day. But don't worry about it," she said off-handedly, "I understand."

He scowled and set aside his menu. "I sometimes forget how direct you can be."

"I'd rather everything was in the open between us. There's no need to concern yourself with what happened. I—needed you, and you were there for me."

His scowl intensified. "In other words, any man would have suited your purposes?"

"No," she said, surprised he'd ask. "Only you. What we shared was very...sweet. I'll always be grateful to you for letting me cry."

"It's not the crying that concerns me."

"The kissing was very special, too," she said softly.

"Yes, I suppose it was. But it might be best to put that, uh, particular part of last night out of our minds."

The waitress approached with pad and pen in hand. They each placed their orders, then Valerie resumed the conversation. "You're welcome to forget the kissing," she said in a mild tone, "but I don't think it'll be that easy for me."

Colby's gaze left hers. "Personally, I don't think I'll be able to forget it, either," he said.

They both fell silent but a faint smile curved her lips as she savored his words. He'd tried to dismiss the attraction between them and couldn't. Neither could she.

"It doesn't change anything," he told her, his voice calm and resolute.

He'd meant everything he'd said earlier; that much Valerie understood clearly now. She couldn't change who she was. Easy as it would be to fall in love with him, Valerie knew she'd never be truly happy as a homemaker. She had too much ambition, too many dreams. A business career was what she wanted, what she did best, and she couldn't relinquish that any more than Colby could give up his medical practice.

"Your father's doing remarkably well," Colby told her in an obvious attempt to change the subject.

Valerie was delighted. Norah had told her repeatedly what excellent progress their father was making, and it was thrilling to have it confirmed.

"I've got him listed as critical at the moment," Colby went on, "but I have a strong feeling that he's going to surprise us all and live to be a hundred."

Valerie beamed Colby a happy smile, hardly able to speak for the emotion clogging her throat. "We owe you so much, Colby."

He brushed off her words and seemed grateful that the waitress appeared just then to deliver their meal.

The soup was delicious, but after a few spoonfuls and only a taste of her fettuccine Valerie was finished, her appetite gone. Colby glanced over, frowning, when she pushed the plate aside.

"Is something wrong?"

She shook her head. "No."

"You barely touched your meal."

"I know."

"What's wrong?" he pressed.

Valerie lowered her eyes. "I was just trying to decide how I was going to leave you, Colby, and not cry." She hadn't meant to sound quite so serious; she'd meant to sound light and wryly amused.

Her words silenced him. His steady gaze met hers, and when he spoke, his voice revealed his sincerity. "You'd be very easy to love."

"But." She said the dreaded word for him.

"But we both know it wouldn't work."

"You're right," she said, convincingly enough. Only why wouldn't her heart listen?

"VALERIE." Her father smiled weakly as she entered the cubicle in SICU. His hand reached for hers, brought it to his lips. "I wondered when I'd see you."

"I . . . went out for dinner."

"All by yourself?"

"No." But she didn't want to tell him she'd been with Colby.

Besides, there were other matters to discuss. Norah had met Valerie with the most unbelievable story. Apparently while Valerie was out for dinner, their father had told Norah about a vision he'd had. A vision? Valerie didn't know what to make of the story, any more than Norah did.

"What's all this Norah was telling me?" she asked gently.

Once again her father smiled, only this time it was brighter and a sparkle appeared in his tired eyes. "I died, you know. Ask Colby if you don't believe me."

Vaguely Valerie remembered Colby saying something about her father's heart stopping and restarting, and considering it a miracle. "I know we're very fortunate to have you with us."

"More fortunate than you realize. Now, I don't want you getting all excited the way your sister did, but then I don't expect you will. I had what those television reporters call a near-death experience."

"The long dark tunnel with the light at the end?" Valerie had heard about the phenomenon herself and knew that Norah probably had, as well.

"Nope," he said, shaking his head. "I was in a garden."

"The Garden of Eden?" Valerie asked lightly.

"Might have been. I couldn't say."

He hadn't realized she was joking. "I didn't notice the trees so much, but there might have been an apple. What I did notice was the pretty woman tending the roses."

"Mom?" Valerie breathed the question, hardly knowing where it came from.

David smiled and shut his eyes. "We had a good, long talk, your mother and I. She convinced me it wasn't my time to die, that there was still plenty for me to do on this good earth. I wasn't pleased to hear it because I've been thinking for some time now that I'd rather be with her."

"Daddy, I don't think—"

"Shush now, because I have lots to tell you and I'm getting weaker by the minute."

"All right."

"Your mother loves you and is very proud of everything you've accomplished, but she told me to tell you to take time to enjoy life before it passes you by."

That sounded like something her mother would say.

"She also told me I was an old fool to try and match you up with Colby."

"But—" She snapped her mouth closed, unwilling to say more.

"Grace feels my pushing the two of you to marry was a ridiculous thing to do. Said I should apologize for that."

Valerie remained silent.

"There was more," David continued, "lots more. Grace wanted to be sure she gave me plenty of reasons to come back to this world."

"I'm very glad she succeeded in convincing you."

Her father's eyes drifted shut, but he opened them again with apparent effort. "She talked to me about Stephanie and Norah, too."

"Good, Daddy," she said softly, patting his hand. "You can tell me all about it next time."

"Want to explain now . . ."

"Shh, sleep."

"You're all going to marry. Your mother assured me all three of you would."

"Of course we will. Eventually."

"Soon. Very . . . soon."

"I'm glad," she whispered, although she wasn't sure he heard her.

So her father had gone through a near-death experience. Valerie didn't know how much credence to put into what he was saying. Marriage was the farthest thing from her mind at the moment. Obviously, marrying Colby was out of the question. And she'd lost interest in the idea of a relationship with Rowdy Cassidy.

"She gave me twelve reasons to live," her father announced sleepily. "Twelve very good reasons."

Valerie recalled that Norah had said something about the number six. She couldn't imagine why her father was speaking in figures all of a sudden.

"Twelve reasons," Valerie echoed, then leaned forward to kiss his cheek.

Her father's eyes fluttered open and he grinned boyishly. "Yup, my grandchildren. You, my darling Valerie, are going to give me three. All within the next few years."

CHAPTER SIX

"WHEN WAS THE LAST TIME you spoke to your father?" Colby asked Valerie when she arrived at the hospital the following morning, carrying an armful of apple blossoms for the nurses' station. He seemed to be waiting for her, and none too patiently.

She sighed, realizing what must have happened. "I take it Dad told you about his experience in the Garden of Eden?"

"It was the Garden of Eden?"

"Figuratively, I suppose."

"So you know, then," Colby muttered. A hint of a frown flickered across his expression.

"Look at it this way—at least Dad's given up his matchmaking efforts." Valerie had assumed Colby would be happy about that, so his reaction puzzled her.

His scowl deepened. "He apologized for even making the suggestion."

"See, what'd I tell you?" Valerie said, her mouth quirking with a smile. "We're both in the clear."

Apparently, this wasn't what Colby wanted to hear, either. "He also claimed you'd be married before the end of the summer—and that you'd promptly present him with three grandchildren."

"In the next few years. It looks like I'm going to be busy, doesn't it?" Valerie hadn't take her father's announcement too seriously; he'd had some kind of pleasant hallucination, she supposed, and if it made him feel better, if it gave him a reason for living, then that was fine. She'd go along with it, though she wouldn't actively encourage him.

Besides, it was highly unlikely she'd marry anytime soon, and even if she did, she had no intention of leaping into this motherhood business. Marriage would be enough of an adjustment. She enjoyed children, and naturally assumed that if she married she'd eventually want a family, but certainly not in the first year or two following her marriage.

"Did he say *who* you're supposed to marry?"

"No. He wouldn't tell Norah, either, although he seemed to enjoy letting her know that she's going to give him six grandchildren. Three boys and three girls. You don't really believe any of this, do you?"

His mouth twisted into a wry grin. "That would be ridiculous, only... Never mind," he finished abruptly.

"No, tell me."

He shrugged, clearly regretting that he'd said anything. "Another patient of mine, an older woman, had a near-death experience. It was all rather... strange."

"She came back convinced she knew who her children would marry and how many grandchildren she was going to have?" Valerie asked sarcastically.

"No." Colby threw her an annoyed glance.

"What happened?" She was curious now, unable to disguise her interest.

"She seemed to know certain things about the future. She—predicted, I guess is the word—certain political events. She wasn't entirely sure how she knew, she just did."

"I'm not sure I understand."

Colby clearly wasn't comfortable outlining the details of his patient's experience. "She didn't have any more than an eighth-grade education, and she'd never had much interest in history or politics. But following the near-death phenomenon she was suddenly able to discuss complicated world problems with genuine insight and skill. She didn't understand it herself, and I certainly didn't have any medical explanation to offer her. The whole thing was as much a mystery to me as it was to her."

Until then, Valerie had to admit, she'd found her father's experience somewhat...entertaining. She'd been willing to tolerate it, since whatever had happened had been very real to her father. This "dreamtime" with her mother had given his life a new purpose, and she was grateful for that, if nothing else.

"What are you saying?" she asked Colby.

"I don't actually know."

Suddenly none of this seemed quite as amusing. "Dad insists I'll be married before the end of the summer."

"He told me the same thing," Colby said. "Is it feasible? I mean, is there someone back in Texas you're seeing on a regular basis?" He gripped his hands behind his back and strolled slowly down the corridor. "Someone other than this person you were hoping to date soon?"

She puffed out her cheeks with air, debating how much to tell him about Rowdy Cassidy. "Not really, but..."

"Go on," he urged when she hesitated.

"My boss, Rowdy Cassidy." She shifted the spray of apple blossoms, conscious of their heady aroma in the antiseptic-smelling hospital corridor.

"The owner of CHIPS?"

Valerie nodded. "I've never actually gone out on a formal date with him, although until recently we saw each other nearly every day. We've traveled together, and frequently attend business dinners together. It wasn't until I arrived here and Dad started talking about you and me marrying that—I don't know, but Rowdy seems the natural choice for me. He's as dedicated to his career as I am and...we get along well."

"He's a wealthy man. Prominent in his field."

"Yes."

Colby's jaw clenched as though he disapproved.

"Do you know something about Rowdy I don't?"

"I've never met the man. Everything I know about him I've read in the newspapers. But from all outward appearances, the two of you should be an ideal couple." His words were indifferent. Then without saying anything more, he turned and walked away from her.

"Colby," Valerie called, once she'd recovered from her initial surprise. She hurried after him. "What's wrong? You're acting like I've done something to offend you."

"I'm not angry," he said, his voice low. His gaze held hers with a disturbing intensity. "I remember what you said yesterday about wondering how we were going to say goodbye. I was just thinking the same thing. I don't know how I'm going to be able to stand by and watch you marry another man."

To her the solution was simple. He could marry her himself. But they'd both already decided that wouldn't work.

"What about you?" she asked, needing to know. "Is there someone special you've been seeing?"

"Yes."

Her heart felt as if it had done a nosedive, colliding with her stomach. Her face must have revealed her shock because he elaborated.

"Sherry Waterman. I thought Norah might have mentioned her."

"A nurse?"

Colby nodded. "She has her nursing degree and she's also trained as a midwife. That's what she's been doing for the past five years. She's good with children and she enjoys weaving and gardening." His voice was brisk and matter-of-fact as he listed Sherry's qualifications.

"She . . . sounds exactly right for you." The aching admission was torn from her throat. Although it was painful to think of Colby with another woman, Valerie knew he'd chosen well in Sherry Waterman. Domestic, talented, perfect in all the ways Valerie wasn't.

"We've been dating for the last year."

"A year," Valerie repeated slowly, surprised he hadn't swept Sherry off her feet long before now. "You shouldn't keep her waiting then."

"I keep telling myself the same thing."

His words hurt, although Valerie pretended otherwise. "I'm delighted for you, Colby."

"Rowdy Cassidy will make you a good husband." His eyes, dark and intense, probed hers.

Valerie smiled and nodded, then they both turned and walked in opposite directions. And although she was tempted, she didn't look back.

"VALERIE, IT'S ROWDY. Thought I'd check and see how everything's going with your father. No one's heard from you in a while."

When had she last reported into CHIPS headquarters? Two days before, she decided. Two whole days! Valerie found that hard to believe. Until recently, her job had been the most important thing in her life, but it wasn't that way now. She'd completely overlooked her responsibilities, forgotten everything that had once been so important. It seemed impossible that she could have allowed so much time to slip past.

"My father had open-heart surgery."

"I understand. How's he doing now?"

"Fabulously well. His recovery in the last twenty-four hours has been remarkable." She didn't tell him that much of the improvement was a result of a change in attitude. Since his "conversation in the garden" with Grace, David Bloomfield's will to live was stronger than ever. If there was something to worry about now, it was the fact that Steffie hadn't arrived yet and no one had heard a word from her. Valerie had spent part of the morning calling the airlines to find out which flight she was on, but to no avail.

"We miss you around here," Rowdy said in that casual way of his. Valerie could picture him sitting in his office, leaning back in his plush leather chair, cowboy boots propped on the mahogany desk. She couldn't remember ever seeing Rowdy without his boots and hat. She always thought of him as the Texan of frontier legend, the man who tackled life with robust energy, who considered no problem insurmountable. He worked hard, played hard and lived hard.

"I miss CHIPS, too."

"Any idea when you'll be back?"

"I'm sorry, no, but if you need me because of the Old West Bank deal—"

"No, no," Rowdy said, breaking in. "We're handling that from our end, so don't you worry about a thing. I just wanted you to know I missed you."

The personal pronoun didn't escape Valerie's notice. Rowdy *was* attracted to her. "My father wanted me to thank you for the flowers," she said. "Th-they got here yesterday morning." She'd hardly noticed at the time, although the nurses had all exclaimed over the lavish bouquets. Now, she felt flustered and nervous with him, something that had never happened before. Their relationship was moving into new territory, and Valerie found the ground unstable and a bit frightening.

"Actually the flowers were for you. I thought you needed something to brighten up your day."

"It was very thoughtful of you."

"It's the least I could do for my favorite executive. You hurry back, you hear?"

"I will. And, Rowdy, thanks for calling." She replaced the phone, and let her breath escape in a deep sigh.

Norah was already in the waiting room when Valerie returned there. "That was Rowdy Cassidy," she explained unnecessarily.

"Are you in love with him?" Norah asked without preamble. "I thought you and Dr. Winston might be hitting it off, but . . ." She let the rest fade.

"Colby's already involved with Sherry Waterman." Valerie kept her voice steady, making a strenuous effort to feign disinterest.

One glance at Norah told her she hadn't succeeded. "You'll notice I never bothered to mention Sherry. There's a reason."

"Oh?" Valerie shrugged. "I wondered . . . I mean, even Colby seemed to think you had, or rather that you should have." She'd wanted to ask her sister earlier, but had hesitated, almost preferring not to know.

"Those two have been dating for almost a year. If Colby was serious about Sherry he would have asked her to marry him before now. Even Sherry's given up on them, although Colby doesn't seem to have figured that out yet. The last thing I heard, she was seeing someone else. Not that I blame her," Norah was quick to add. "It must be the most frustrating thing in the world to be crazy about a guy and have him lukewarm toward you."

"I'm sure it must be."

"You still haven't answered me," Norah pressed. "What about Rowdy? Are you in love with him?"

Valerie shrugged again, uncomfortable with the subject of her boss, unsure of her own feelings toward him. "Yes and no."

"You're beginning to sound like Colby. I think he loves everything Sherry represents. She's a nurturing, kind-hearted woman. She fits the image of what Colby wants in a wife."

"Then what's stopping him?"

Norah gnawed on her lower lip for several moments. "My guess is that she bores him. Don't get me wrong, Sherry's not a colorless kind of person. Actually when I think about it, Sherry and I are a lot alike. She's a homebody like me, and little things mean a lot to her. She doesn't need an active social life or fancy clothes. Given the choice between a stay-at-home date with a rented movie or dining in a world-class restaurant, she'd opt for the movie."

"I see."

"You're much better suited to Colby."

"Me?" Valerie asked, her voice rising in astonishment. Hadn't Norah just finished describing the kind of woman Colby wanted—a woman completely unlike Valerie?

"I've seen the looks the two of you exchange," Norah continued, looking thoughtful. "I'm not blind, you know. I feel the electricity whenever I'm with you. It's mutual and it's hot."

"Really," Valerie said, becoming preoccupied with the crease in her wool slacks.

"Yes, really!"

"Yes, well, we've decided differently. We're attracted to each other, but nothing's going to come of it." She glanced at her watch, wanting an excuse to leave. "I'm going to stop in and see Dad."

Norah's smile seemed all-knowing. "Okay."

David Bloomfield's color was better, and he grinned happily when he saw his eldest daughter.

"Hello, Dad," she said in a cheerful voice as she bent over to kiss his cheek.

"Valerie," he whispered, holding out his hand to her. "Listen, sweetheart, you're spending too much time here at the hospital. Take the day and get out in the sunshine. You're beginning to look pale."

"But..."

"It'll do you good. No more sleeping on some dilapidated couch here at the hospital, either."

She'd slept in her own bed in her own room for the first time the night before. In the morning, she'd been amazed at how well rested she felt. And she'd indulged in a long, hot shower, followed by a good breakfast—cooked by Norah, needless to say.

The crews were just beginning to spray the apple trees and she'd heard the familiar sounds of men busy working in the orchards. It brought back memories of years past, of racing down the long, even rows, and climbing onto the low limbs of the trees, sitting there like a princess surveying her magical kingdom. Orchard Valley *was* magical, a town set apart in time.

For Valerie, coming home was like escaping to the past. The people were friendly, the neighbors neighborly, and problems were shared. It was a little piece of heaven.

"I wasn't at the hospital last night," she told him, pulling herself from her musings. She loved Orchard Valley more than any place on earth, but she'd never be content living here. There wasn't enough challenge, enough to tax her mind. No, Texas was her future and she accepted that with only one regret. Colby.

"So I heard," her father answered. "I saw Colby earlier."

Valerie watched his expression, hoping for— what?—some sign, some indication of her father's thoughts. And of Colby's... There was none.

"Well? What did the good doctor have to say?"

"Nothing much."

"Did he mention me?" she couldn't prevent herself from asking.

"Nope, I can't say he did. Does that disappoint you?"

"Of course not."

"Is there any reason he should mention you to me?"

Valerie was sorry she'd brought up the subject. "Not that I know of."

Her answers seemed to make him smile. "So you like my doctor?"

"He's been wonderful to you," Valerie agreed.

"I wasn't talking about me," David answered gruffly. "I'm referring to you. You're attracted to him, aren't you, Valerie? You never were much good at disguising your feelings."

"I've never met a man who appeals to me more," Valerie said truthfully. There was no point in trying to deceive her father. He knew her all too well, and he understood her better than anyone, sometimes better than she understood herself.

"He feels the same way?" The question was gentle, as though he were speaking to a child.

Valerie lowered her eyes before shaking her head. "It'd never work, and we both know it."

She expected an argument from her father, was even looking for one. She wanted him to tell her she was wrong, that love could work when two people were committed to each other. That it wouldn't matter how dissimilar they were, how differently they viewed life. That nothing mattered but the love they shared...

Her father, however, said nothing.

Discouraged, Valerie said a quick goodbye and returned to the waiting room. On her way, she noticed that Norah sat talking to another doctor at the end of the hallway. She was grateful her sister had left, because she needed time alone to think.

If she was looking for evidence that people with very different personalities could fall in love and make the relationship work, she need look no further than her own parents. The story of how they'd met and fallen in love was like a fairy tale, one that, as a child, she'd never tired of hearing.

Her father had fought in the Korean War. Afterward, he'd gone to university on the G.I. Bill and obtained his degree in business administration. Armed with his dreams, he'd built a financial empire and became a millionaire within a matter of years. Then he'd collapsed with rheumatic fever, nearly losing his life. It was while he was in the hospital recuperating that he'd met a young nurse. David knew the moment he

met Grace Johnson that he was going to love her. It
never occurred to him that she would refuse his marriage proposal.

It took him several months of relentless pursuit to
convince Grace to marry him. Despite the fact that she
was deeply in love with David, Grace had been afraid.
She was a preacher's daughter who'd lived a simple
life. David was a business tycoon who'd taken auto-
mation technology to new industry heights. Grace's
fears about a marriage to David Bloomfield were well
warranted. But over the years, love had proven even
the most hardened skeptics wrong, and the two had
lived and loved together until her mother's death a few
years before.

Her own romance wasn't going to have a fairy-tale
ending, the way her parents' had. Her father knew it,
too, otherwise he would have been the first to encourage her.

Her father, however, had said nothing.

VALERIE WAS WORKING in the den, putting her CHIPS
files in order, when she saw the red car hurtle down the
driveway. She thought, for one hopeful moment, that
it might be Colby, but then remembered he drove a
maroon Buick. Still, she hastened to answer the door.

It was Charles Tomaselli, looking tired and frus-
trated.

"Have you heard anything from Stephanie?" he
demanded without so much as a greeting.

Her sister's absence had been weighing on Valerie's
mind, too. She'd done everything she could think of;

she'd even placed a call to the American Embassy in Rome, with no results.

"I haven't heard a word. I don't know what could have happened to her."

"How late is she?"

Valerie had to think for a moment. In the past week, she'd lost all track of time. "Norah was the last person to speak to Steffie," she explained. "Let me see— that was just before Dad's surgery. Steffie thought she'd be home within twenty-four hours."

"That was forty-eight hours ago."

He didn't need to remind her, Valerie thought irritably. "She's coming by way of Tokyo."

"Tokyo? She's heading for Oregon by way of *Japan?*" Charles snapped.

"I don't believe she had much choice."

"Don't you think you should be making some inquiries?" he asked gruffly.

"I already have. Tell me who else I should call and I'll be happy to do so."

Charles settled down on the top porch step, resting both elbows on his knees. "I don't mind telling you, Valerie, I'm worried. She should have been here before now."

"I know."

"I have some friends, some connections," Charles said absently, "and I've checked with them. But they can't find any trace of her on the scheduled flights out of Rome. If she hasn't arrived by tomorrow afternoon, I don't think you have any alternative but to contact the authorities."

Valerie swallowed tightly, then nodded. She could just slap Steffie silly for putting them through all this worry.

"She's okay, Charles," Valerie said after a moment.

"What makes you so sure?" He turned to look up at her.

"I . . . don't know, I just am."

Charles stood agilely, his gaze leveled on the long narrow driveway that led in from the road. "I hope you're right, Valerie. I hope you're right."

NORAH CAME BACK from the hospital a half hour later, talkative and lively. "I can't get over how much Dad's improved in such a short time."

Valerie took the shrimp salad she'd prepared for their dinner from the refrigerator. Salads were her specialty. That, and folding napkins. She could do both without a hitch.

For the first time since her arrival, Valerie had spent most of the day away from the hospital. When her father had suggested she leave, she'd initially felt a bit piqued. But as she revisited the life that had once been hers in this quiet community, she accepted the wisdom of his words. She *had* needed to get out, to breathe in the serenity she found in Orchard Valley and exhale the fear that had choked her from the moment she'd received Norah's frantic message. Then, after her walk, she'd come back to the house, and because she'd never been idle in her life, she'd set up a communications center in her father's den.

"I'm going back to work, starting tomorrow," Norah announced between bites of lettuce, shrimp and slices of hard-boiled egg. "The hospital's understaffed, but then when isn't it? I'll still be able to see Dad, maybe even more often than before. You don't mind, do you?"

"Of course I don't mind. You do whatever you think best."

"You're not going to leave, are you?" Norah asked, rushing the words together. "I wouldn't do this if the hospital didn't need me so badly."

"I realize that."

Norah sampled another forkful of salad. "You're quiet tonight. Is anything wrong?"

"Not really." She didn't want to worry Norah about Steffie's disappearance.

"Colby asked about you."

She felt her stomach churn with contradictory emotions. Part of her was thrilled that he'd even mentioned her, yet she experienced a growing sense of apprehension, too.

"He wanted to know where you were."

"Did you tell him?"

"Of course," Norah answered blithely. "He said he thought it was a good idea for you to get out of the hospital more. You've practically been living there ever since you arrived." She slowly chewed another bite of her salad. "He asked me what I knew about Rowdy Cassidy," she said casually.

Valerie put down her fork, her appetite having fled. "What did you tell him?"

"The truth. That I've never met the man, but Dad seems to think he's wonderful. You probably weren't aware of this, but Dad's been following CHIPS ever since you started working there. He thinks Rowdy's a genius. Funny, though—I got the impression that wasn't what Colby wanted to hear."

"The shrimp was on sale at Vern's Market," Valerie said, changing the subject abruptly, not wanting to talk about Colby. Not now when she felt so vulnerable, so conscious of the attraction between them. "Vern said he cooked it himself this morning."

"You don't want to talk about Colby?"

Valerie grinned. Her sister hadn't graduated magna cum laude for nothing.

"You're not going any place tonight, are you?" Norah asked next.

"I thought I'd drive in to the hospital and visit Dad, but other than that, no. What did you have in mind? Do you need me to do something?"

Norah shrugged. "I may be wrong, but I think Colby wanted to talk to you. I have a feeling he might call."

Norah was right.

When Valerie returned from her trip to the hospital, her sister had left a note taped to her bedroom door.

COLBY PHONED. SAID HE'D TALK TO YOU IN THE MORNING.

Valerie read the message with mixed feelings. Thrill and dread went at it for round two, again evenly matched. She determined to forget everything—love, Colby, the future—for tonight. The morning would be soon enough to resume her worries. She craved the forgetfulness of sleep, the escape from thought and feeling.

Valerie had assumed she'd fall asleep with the same ease she had the previous night. For a solid hour she beat her pillow, tossed and turned in an effort to find a comfortable position. Finally giving up, she reached for the light on the bed stand and read until her eyes drifted shut and the business journal slipped from her fingers.

But Valerie's exhausted sleep wasn't the restful oblivion she'd longed for. Colby wandered into her mind like an uninvited guest.

He looked devilishly handsome, dressed in the suit he'd worn the night he'd taken her to the Italian restaurant.

"You're not going to be able to forget me, are you?"

In her dream, Valerie said nothing, but only because she had no argument. She merely stared at him, adoring every feature, every movement.

A noise disturbed her, distracting her from Colby. Irritated, she looked over her shoulder to see what it was and when she looked back, he was gone. She cried out in frustration, the sound of her own voice jerking her awake. She was sitting upright in the bed, heart pounding furiously.

It took her another moment to realize there was some sort of commotion going on downstairs. She climbed out of bed and grabbed her robe.

From the top of the stairs, she saw Norah, laughing and crying at once. A battered-looking suitcase stood on the floor, along with a leather coat and an umbrella.

"Steffie!" Valerie cried excitedly, racing down the stairs.

Her sister was home.

CHAPTER SEVEN

COLBY CHECKED the clipboard at the foot of David Bloomfield's bed and scanned the notations the nursing staff had written through the night. Although his gaze was lowered, he couldn't help being aware of David Bloomfield's cocky grin.

"You must be feeling more like your old self this morning," he observed genially.

David's smile widened. "I'm feeling more chipper each and every day. How much longer do you intend to keep me prisoner? I'm itching to get home."

"Another week," Colby answered, replacing the clipboard. "Perhaps less, depending on how well you do."

"A week!" David protested. "Are you sure you aren't holding me up just so you'll have an excuse to visit with Valerie twice a day?"

Colby's hackles rose, and he was about to defend his medical judgment when he realized the old man was baiting him—and enjoying it.

"I'm going to have you transferred out of the Surgical Intensive Care Unit this morning," Colby continued, "but first I want you up and walking."

"I've been up."

Colby glanced back at the chart, surprised to see no indication of the activity.

"I just didn't let anyone know. I felt a bit dizzy, so I only walked around the bed. Not much of a trip, but it tired me out plenty."

"You're not to get out of this bed again unless there's someone with you, understand?" He used his sternnest voice.

"All right, all right," David agreed. Stroking his chin, he studied Colby. "She's pretty as a picture, that oldest daughter of mine. Isn't she, Doc?"

Colby ignored both the comment and the question. "I'll have one of the nursing staff down in a few minutes and we'll see how well you do with the exercise. I imagine by the end of the day you'll have conquered the hallway."

"From what I hear, that Rowdy Cassidy's been calling her two, three times a day."

Colby stiffened at the mention of the other's man name. He'd tried to tell himself that Valerie would be happier married to Cassidy. They shared the same attitudes, beliefs and ambitions; together they'd take the business world by storm. Rowdy was exactly the type of dynamic personality who'd help Valerie fulfill her goals and dreams. She'd never be content as a physician's wife. He knew it. And she knew it. Nevertheless Colby was having trouble accepting the obvious.

He'd never thought of himself as romantic. His career had consumed his life from the time he was a high-school sophomore. His much-loved grandfather had died of heart disease, and it was then that Colby had decided to become a doctor. Everything else in his life had been subordinated to that goal. Only in the past year or so had he felt the desire to marry and start a family.

He'd acted upon that desire with methodical thoroughness, mentally tabulating a list of his wants and needs. He'd looked around at the single women in Orchard Valley and decided to date Sherry Waterman. If things didn't work out with Sherry, Norah Bloomfield was next on his list, although he was a bit concerned about their age difference.

Things *had* worked out with Sherry, at least in the beginning. He'd found her refreshing and genuine and fun. Problems crept up later, when he realized she was entirely predictable. Involved with a woman who embodied every trait he wanted in his life's partner, he'd been...bored. He wasn't sure anymore that he needed someone quite so even-tempered and domestic.

According to the schedule he'd set for himself, he should have been married by now.

He wasn't.

To irritate him further, the only woman he'd found himself strongly attracted to in the past year was Valerie Bloomfield, and anyone with a lick of sense could see they weren't the least bit compatible.

For months, long before his heart attack, David Bloomfield had found excuses to drag his eldest daughter's name into their conversations. By the time he met Valerie, Colby was thoroughly sick of hearing about her. He hadn't even expected to *like* her. Instead, his heart and his head had been spinning out of control from that first moment.

It was time to put an end to such nonsense, before either of them took this attraction business too seriously.

"Cassidy would be a good match for a woman like Valerie," he said as offhandedly as he could. The last thing he wanted was for Valerie's father to know how attracted he was to her, though he suspected David already knew. The old man seemed to have a sixth sense about such matters.

"Rowdy will, at that," David returned matter-of-factly. "I should know, too." The cocky grin was back in place.

Colby's chest tightened, his anger brewing just beneath the surface. David hadn't mentioned his dream lately, the one he'd termed his near-death experience. But from bits and pieces of conversation, Colby had learned that David was still predicting Valerie's wedding. It made sense that the man he expected her to marry was Rowdy Cassidy.

All the better, damn it. He—

"Stephanie's home," David continued conversationally, cutting into Colby's thoughts. "I saw her briefly this morning. What a lovely sight she was to these tired eyes."

Colby nodded, finding it difficult to dispel the image of Valerie married to her employer. Well, he'd better get used to the idea, because it was likely to happen soon. And because he refused to deliberately ruin his life by marrying the wrong woman.

He'd call Sherry this afternoon, Colby decided with renewed determination, and ask her out to dinner. One thing was certain; he intended to steer clear of Valerie Bloomfield, no matter how hard that was.

So much for the best laid plans, Colby mused as he left the Surgical Intensive Care Unit. Valerie was standing in the corridor waiting for him. As always, when he first saw her, his heart gladdened. An old-fashioned expression, perhaps, but he didn't know how else to describe what came over him when he was with Valerie.

He remembered the time he'd sought her out after losing Joanna Murphy. Just being with her had taken the sharp edge off the pain of that unexpected death, had helped him deal with the frustration, the sense of powerlessness. When she'd suggested coffee, his first inclination had been to refuse, but he'd found he couldn't. Sharing his concerns with her had, in some indefinable way, comforted him.

It seemed to him that their conversation had helped her, too, in coming to terms with her father's illness.

They'd helped each other. In thinking about those moments together, Colby understood why he couldn't simply dismiss his fascination with her as sexual attraction. That was part of it, all right. But more than any woman he'd ever known, Valerie Bloomfield was his equal. In intelligence, in emotional strength, in commitment to those she loved.

Every time Colby had been with her since, he experienced an elation, a small joy that left him feeling bewildered. Left him wanting to be with her more and more. Yet he knew he couldn't afford to pursue a relationship that had no chance of lasting.

"You wanted to see me?" Valerie asked, her gaze meeting his expectantly.

He frowned and shook his head. "No."

"Norah left a note for me last night, saying you'd phoned."

"Oh, that. It was nothing." He wanted to kick himself for that phone call now. He'd been looking for a reason to talk to her. His day had been long and tiring, and his defenses down, so he'd made up an excuse to hear the sound of her voice.

"I just wanted to tell you I'm transferring your father from SICU this morning," he went on quickly. "His progress has been nothing short of remarkable. If it continues like this, he'll be out of the hospital inside a week."

Valerie's eyes sparkled with relief. "That's wonderful news! It seems everything's happening at once. I don't know if you heard, but Steffie got home last night."

"So I understand." Colby watched her closely. Although she said nothing more, he realized that something was troubling Valerie. Her brow had furrowed, ever so briefly, when she mentioned her sister's name. Colby was convinced she wasn't aware of the tiny, telltale action.

"Something happened with your sister?"

Her eyes widened in surprise. "Yes, just now. She was sitting in the waiting room reading a copy of the *Clarion* when she leaped to her feet, demanding to know if I'd read it. Before I could say anything, she left, taking the newspaper with her. I can't remember ever seeing Steffie so angry. I'm not sure what got into her, but I'm guessing it has something to do with Charles Tomaselli."

"I'm sure she'll tell you eventually."

"I'm sure she will, too, though I have a sneaking suspicion this is connected to a news article he wrote with Dad's help. I just don't understand what she found so offensive. Those two can't seem to get along. They never could. It's always surprised me, because she seemed to be so keen on him."

The temptation to linger, even to suggest they have coffee together, was strong, but Colby resisted. He was doing a lot of that where Valerie was concerned. Resisting. He only hoped his willpower held firm until she went back to Texas—and to Cassidy—where she belonged.

"VALERIE," Steffie said, standing in the doorway outside Valerie's bedroom. "Have you got a moment?"

"Sure." Valerie was sitting up in bed reading, but her mind wasn't on the latest computer technology she'd had every intention of studying. With infuriating frequency, her thoughts drifted away from super-resolution monitors and narrowed in on Colby. She welcomed her sister's visit, not least as a distraction.

Steffie crossed the room and sat on the edge of Valerie's bed. "I made a complete fool of myself this morning," she admitted, her eyes downcast.

Valerie waited for her to explain, but further details didn't seem to be forthcoming. Her curiosity was aroused, but she didn't want to pry.

"With Charles," Steffie finally said, drawing her knees up and circling them with her arms. "It isn't the first time, either. He's the one person in the world I swore I never wanted to speak to again and the first few hours I'm home, I make a complete idiot of myself over him."

Valerie set aside her business journal and drew up her own knees. "He's been worried about you."

"You've talked to him? When? What did he say?" Steffie's head came up. Her long dark hair fell to the middle of her back, and her eyes, so dark and earnest, probed Valerie's. Although Steff was twenty-four, she looked closer to sixteen. Especially now, when she felt so embarrassed and unsure.

"I haven't talked to him recently. Charles asked about you shortly after I got home, and later he was concerned because you didn't arrive when we expected you. Apparently he made some inquiries, trying to track you down. Both Norah and I were so caught up in what was happening with Dad that we weren't as concerned about your late appearance as we should have been. Charles, however, seemed terribly anxious."

"He was just hoping I'd get home in time to make an idiot of myself, which I did."

Valerie thought that was unfair of Steffie. "Charles has been wonderful," she protested.

"To you and Norah. I'm the one he can't get along with." Steffie's shoulders rose as she gave a deep, heartfelt sigh. "How do you know when you're in love, really in love?" she asked plaintively.

Their mother should be the one answering that question. Not Valerie. She hadn't figured out her relationships with Colby *or* Rowdy. Bemused, she shook her head. She could outsmart the competition, bring down some of the biggest deals in the industry, but she didn't know how to tell if she was in love.

"I wish I could answer that myself," Valerie said quietly. "I know next to nothing about love. I was sort of hoping you'd be able to enlighten me."

Steffie frowned. "Don't tell me we're going to have to go to Norah about this."

"We can't," Valerie said, then started to laugh.

"What's so funny? Listen, Val, this isn't a time for humor, or pride, for that matter. If Norah knows more than we do, which she probably does, then we should forget she's the youngest and come right out and ask her."

"We can't ask Norah about love, because she isn't here," Valerie explained. "She's out on a date."

Steffie started to laugh, too, not because it was particularly funny, but because it was a rare moment of shared closeness between sisters.

"Reading between the lines of your letters, I assumed you'd fallen in love with your boss," she said next. "You never admitted it, but the two of you seemed to be spending a lot of time together."

"I think I might have been half in love with him until I met Colby."

"Dad's heart doctor?"

Valerie nodded. "When I first arrived home, Dad was fully expecting to die. He actually seemed to be looking forward to it, which annoyed everyone. Although not being able to get home must have been a nightmare for you, it might well be the one thing that kept him hanging on as long as he did."

"You're sidestepping the issue. Tell me about Colby."

"It started with Dad's matchmaking efforts, which I found rather amusing and Colby found utterly frustrating, but then as we got to know each other we realized there was a spark." More of a blowtorch than a spark, really, but she wasn't going to say so.

"If you're in love with Colby, then why do you look like you're going to cry?"

"Because we both know it wouldn't work. He's a small-town doctor, who occasionally lectures at Portland University. Although he could practice anywhere, he wants to stay right here in Orchard Valley."

"And you don't?"

"I don't think I could be happy here," Valerie said miserably. "Not anymore. And there are other problems, too..."

"But if you truly loved each other, you'd be able to find a solution to your differences."

"That's just it. I don't know if this *is* love, and I don't think Colby does, either. Everything would be so much easier if we did.

"I'm attracted to him. I think about him constantly, but is that enough for me to forsake all my ambitions? Give up my career? I don't know, Steffie, and it's got me tied up in knots. How do I decide? And if I *did* quit CHIPS and found some other job around here, how do I know I wouldn't resent him five years down the road? How do I know he wouldn't end up resenting me for not being a more traditional kind of woman—which is what he wants? Besides, even if I do love Colby, how can I be sure he feels the same way about me?''

"I wish Mom was here."

"So do I," Valerie said fervently. "Oh, Steffie, so do I."

VALERIE DIDN'T SEE Colby for several days. Four, to be exact. As her father's health improved, she spent less and less time at the hospital, therefore decreasing her chances of casually bumping into him. She was working out of the house, and that helped. Being in a familiar place, doing familiar tasks, alloyed her fears and tempered her frustrations.

She knew she should think about returning to Texas. The crisis had passed, and by remaining in Orchard Valley she was creating one of a different sort. CHIPS, Inc., needed her. Rowdy Cassidy needed her. She'd already missed one important business trip, and though Rowdy had encouraged her to stay in Orchard Valley as long as necessary, he'd also let her know he was looking forward to her return.

Valerie had almost run out of excuses to remain in Oregon. Her father was scheduled to be discharged in record time and Valerie, with her two sisters, planned a celebration dinner that included Colby.

She was surprised he'd accepted the invitation. Surprised and pleased. She was hungry for the sight of him. He was in her thoughts constantly, and she couldn't help wondering if it was the same for him.

All afternoon, she'd been feeling like a schoolgirl. Excited and nearly giddy at the prospect of her father's return—especially since Colby would be driving him back home.

Norah had been in the kitchen most of the afternoon. Since Valerie's culinary skills were limited to salad preparation and napkin folding, she'd been assigned both jobs, along with setting the table.

"What time is it?" Steffie called from the kitchen.

Valerie, who was carefully arranging their best china on the dining-room table, shot a glance toward the grandfather clock. "Five."

"They're due in less than thirty minutes."

"Do I detect a note of panic?" Valerie teased.

"Dinner isn't even close to being done," Steffie told her.

They'd chosen a menu that included none of their father's favorites. David Bloomfield was a meat-and-potatoes man, but that was all about to change. Colby had been very definite. From here on, David would be a low-cholesterol-and-high-fiber man.

"The dining-room table's set," Valerie informed the others. To the best of her memory, it was the first time they'd brought out the china since their mother's death. But their father's welcome-home dinner warranted using the very best.

Fifteen minutes later, Valerie glanced out the living-room window to see Colby's maroon car coming down the long driveway. "They're here!" she shouted, hurrying to the front porch, barely able to contain her excitement.

This moment seemed like a miracle to her. She'd come to accept that she was going to lose her father, and now he'd been given a second chance at life. Gratitude filled her heart. This was so much more than she'd dared hope.

Steffie and Norah joined her on the porch. Colby climbed out of the car first and came around to assist David. It was all Valerie could do not to rush down the steps and help him herself. Although her father had made phenomenal progress in the eight days since his surgery, he remained terribly pale and thinner than she'd ever seen him. But his eyes glowed with obvious pride and satisfaction as he looked on his three daughters.

He turned to Colby and said something Valerie couldn't hear. Whatever it was made Colby's eyes dart toward Valerie. She met his gaze, all too briefly, then they looked hurriedly away from each other, as though embarrassed to be caught staring.

"I'm afraid dinner's not quite ready," Norah said as Colby eased David into his recliner by the fireplace.

"I've been waiting two weeks for a decent meal," David grumbled. "Hospital food never did sit well with me. I hope you've outdone yourself."

"I have," Norah promised, smiling at Valerie. Their father wasn't expecting poached salmon and dill sauce with salad and rice, but he'd adjust to healthier eating habits soon enough.

"Can I get you anything, Dad?" Valerie asked, expecting him to request the evening paper or a cup of coffee.

"Walk down and see if the Howard boy is still in the orchard, would you, Val?"

"Of course, but I don't think you should be worried about the orchard now."

"I'm not worried. I just want to know what's been going on while I was laid up. I promise I'm not going to overdo it. Colby wouldn't let me. I tried to die three times, but he was right there making sure I didn't. Don't think I'd want to ruin all that effort now, do you?"

Valerie grinned. "All right, I'll check and see if the foreman's still around."

"Colby," David said, raising his index finger imperiously, "you go with her. I don't want her walking in the orchard alone."

The request was a shamefully blatant excuse to throw them together, but neither complained.

Colby followed her out the front door and down the porch steps. "You don't need to come," she said, looking up at him. "I've been walking through these same orchards since I was a toddler. I won't get lost."

"I know that."

"Dad was just inventing a way for us to be alone."

"I know that, too. He told me what he intended when we arrived."

"But why?"

"Isn't it obvious?"

"Yes, but..." Her father had all but announced that he anticipated a prompt wedding between her and Rowdy Cassidy. He seemed downright delighted at the prospect, too, talking about her marriage as if it were a foregone conclusion.

"How have you been?" Colby asked. They strolled in the late-afternoon sunshine toward the west side of the orchard, where the equipment was kept. There was a small office in the storage building, as well, and if Dale Howard was still in the orchard that was the most likely place to find him.

"I've been fine. And you?" Valerie could tell him the truth about her feelings, or a half-truth. She chose the truth. "I've missed you."

Colby clasped his hands behind his back. It might have been wishful thinking on her part, but Valerie thought he did so in an effort to keep from touching her.

"I understand your boss is calling you every day," he said stiffly.

"I understand you took Sherry Waterman out to dinner this week," she returned.

"It didn't help any," he muttered. "The whole time we were together I kept thinking how I'd rather be with you. Is that what you were hoping to hear?"

Valerie dropped her gaze to the soft dirt beneath her feet. "No, but I'll admit I'm glad."

"This isn't going to work."

How rigid his words sounded, as though he was holding himself in check and finding it more and more difficult. "What isn't?"

"You—being here."

"Here? You didn't have to come with me. I've already explained that I'm perfectly capable of finding my way—"

"CHIPS stock went up two dollars a share last week."

Colby was leaping from one subject to the next. "That's wonderful," she said cautiously. "I'm sure Rowdy's thrilled."

"You should be, too."

"As a stockholder myself, I am, but what has that got to do with anything?"

"Houston is where you belong, with Rowdy Cassidy and all his millions."

Rowdy had been telling her the same thing. Not in quite the same words, but he wanted her in Texas. With him. Not a day passed that he didn't let her know how much he missed her. Rowdy wasn't a romantic kind of man; fancy words weren't his forte. He was as straightforward as Valerie herself. He missed her, he said, missed the time they spent together and the discussions they'd shared. He hadn't realized how much until she'd left.

"When are you going back?" Colby demanded.

Valerie realized this was the whole purpose of their being alone together. This was the reason he'd fallen in with her father's schemes and had walked in the orchard with her. He wanted her out of Orchard Valley and out of his life.

"Soon," she promised and her voice cracked with pain. Damn, but it hurt. The intensity of it took her by surprise; embarrassed, she increased her pace to a half trot, wanting to escape.

"Valerie." His voice came from behind her.

"No, please, I understand . . . you're right. I'll—" She wasn't allowed to finish her thought. Colby caught her by the upper arm and turned her to face him, bringing her into his warm embrace.

He drew her wrists up and placed them around his neck as though she were a rag doll, then circled her waist with his arms and brought her tight against him. Before she had a chance to catch her breath, his mouth was on hers.

Valerie felt as though she'd drown in the sheer ecstasy of being in his arms again. It wasn't supposed to be like this. It wasn't supposed to feel so right, so good. His mouth was hungry and eager and she opened to him as naturally as a flower to the sun.

She clung to him, and then he suddenly jerked his head away. Valerie pressed her face into his shoulder and shuddered. She might have been able to forget him, forget these feelings, if he hadn't kissed her again, if he hadn't taken her into his arms.

"Valerie, can't you see what's happening?"

She nodded. "I'm falling in love with you."

"We can't allow this to continue."

"But—"

"Are you willing to risk everything we've both worked all our lives to achieve? Are you going to change, or do you expect me to? The fact is, you know damn well that *neither* of us wants to give anything up.

So we've got to put an end to this. Because, Valerie, we have nothing in common.''

Offhand, Valerie could think of several things they had in common, but she didn't mention them. There was no point. She understood what Colby was saying. If they continued as they were, in each other's arms, it would lead to the inevitable, and they'd be so deeply in love that they'd forget what was keeping them apart. They'd choose to forget that Valerie had a wonderful career waiting for her back in Houston. They'd choose to forget that Colby wanted a woman who'd be a dedicated homemaker. They'd overlook even the most obvious differences. For a while, their love would be enough, but that wouldn't last, not for long. Not long enough.

"It's time to go back," Colby said, releasing her completely.

"Dad won't be worried."

"I'm not talking about your father. I'm talking about you, Valerie. Go back to Texas," he said, his dark eyes holding hers, "before it's too late." He turned and walked away from her then. It was the second time he'd pleaded with her to leave, and this time it hurt even more than it had the first.

CHAPTER EIGHT

"COLBY'S TAKEN Sherry Waterman out three nights in a row," Norah said casually over a cup of coffee early Saturday morning. "They've gone out every night since Dad's been home." She nibbled her toast, but her gaze just managed to avoid Valerie's, as though she felt guilty about relaying the information.

"I take it there's a reason you want me to know this."

"Yes," Norah murmured. "Sherry was at the hospital, and we had a chance to talk. She says she can't understand why Colby keeps asking her out. The spark just isn't there. They enjoy each other's company, but they're never going to be more than friends. It almost seems as if Colby wants to make it into something it's not."

"Perhaps Sherry's reading more into the situation than there is." Valerie didn't actually believe that, but she felt compelled to suggest it. She knew exactly what Colby was doing—escaping her, fighting everything he felt for her.

"Sherry realizes Colby's in love with someone else, and she also knows he's fighting it." Norah's words were an eerie echo of her own thoughts. "It's you, isn't it, Val? Colby's in love with you."

"I can't speak for him," Valerie insisted, munching furiously on her toast.

"Do you love him?"

She gave a tolerant shrug and answered the question with one of her own, always a good business move. "What do I know about love?"

"You know enough," Norah argued. "Please, do everyone a favor and put the poor guy out of his misery."

"How am I supposed to do that?" Valerie asked, genuinely curious. She was miserable, too, but no one seemed to take *that* into consideration. In other circumstances, she would have talked to Steffie, but her younger sister was having relationship problems of her own.

"For the love of heaven," Norah cried, "just marry him. He's crazy about you. Any fool can see that, and you're in love with him, too."

"Sometimes love isn't enough."

"Yes, it is," Norah argued.

Perhaps to Norah, who was young and idealistic, love would be enough, but there were too many complications Valerie couldn't afford to ignore in her relationship with Colby. Besides, he'd been pretty explicit about wanting her to leave.

"I think you should quit your job, move back home and marry Dr. Winston," Norah said decisively.

"And do what?" Valerie asked. "Take up politics? Learn to knit? If I was *really* lucky, I might find some job in town that was about a tenth as interesting as the job I have. Listen, I've been an active businesswoman for the last six years. Do you honestly think

I'd be happy sitting at home knitting sweaters for the rest of my life?''

''You would be in time. It'll take a little adjusting, that's all.''

''Oh, Norah.'' Valerie sighed and gave her starry-eyed sister a pitying smile. ''You make everything sound so simple. It just isn't. Colby isn't exactly pining away for me, not if he's spending all that time with Sherry. If he wants me to stay, he'll ask.''

''What if he doesn't? Are you willing to throw away a chance for happiness because you've got too much pride? You should tell him you're willing to stay, don't you think?'' Norah returned heatedly. ''Why does everything have to come from Colby?''

''It doesn't, believe me. But it's too late.''

''What's too late?'' their father asked from the kitchen doorway. He was dressed in his plaid housecoat, the belt cinched tightly at the waist. He ran a hand down his disheveled hair, looking as though he'd only recently awakened.

Norah automatically stood and guided him to a chair.

''What are you two arguing about?'' he asked. ''I could hear you all the way to the back bedroom.''

Their father was sleeping downstairs because Colby didn't want him climbing stairs yet. Although he hadn't complained, Valerie knew her father was anxious to return to his own room.

''We weren't arguing, Dad,'' Valerie said, ignoring Norah's angry look.

''I heard you,'' David countered, smiling up at Norah as she brought him a cup of coffee. ''It seems to me I heard Norah suggest you should marry Colby. It's the same thing I've been saying for weeks. So has everyone else who's got a nickel's worth of sense.''

Valerie's throat seemed to close up on her. "He has to ask me first. And...and I thought you—Rowdy and I—"

"Phooey. Rowdy Cassidy's a good man, but he's not for you. That was just to get you—and that stubborn doctor—thinking. And as for Colby not asking you, ask him yourself.''

"Dad..." The list of objections was too long to enumerate. The best thing to do was ignore the suggestion, Valerie decided.

"You've never been shy about going after what you want. I've always admired that about you. You love him, don't you? So ask him to marry you. You might be pleasantly surprised by what he says,'' Norah suggested.

"It wouldn't work," Valerie said sadly. "Colby's as traditional as they come. When he's found the woman he wants to marry, he'll propose himself.''

Neither Norah nor her father offered a rebuttal, which suited Valerie. A few minutes later she left the kitchen and wandered up to her room to dress, but she didn't get far. Sitting on the end of her bed, she closed her eyes and tried to think. Was she being unnecessarily stubborn? Was Norah right? Was she allowing pride to stand in the way of happiness? Questions came at her from all directions, and she felt at a loss to answer them.

There seemed to be only one way of finding out what she needed to know and that meant confronting

Colby. For years she'd been working at finding solutions in unlikely situations. It was her greatest strength in business, but when it came to her own life, she drew a blank. There had to be an answer that suited them both, but for now it escaped her.

SHE WAS OBVIOUSLY the last person Colby expected to see when he answered his front door. Valerie saw the astonishment in his eyes and felt encouraged. She'd hoped to catch him off guard and had succeeded.

"Hello, Colby," she said softly.

"Valerie . . . hello."

She'd dressed carefully, taking time to choose the perfect outfit for her purposes. Something that would remind him she was a woman—but not a pushover. She found the solution in a lovely soft pink sweater dress Steffie had brought with her from Italy.

"Would it be all right if I came in for a few moments?" she asked when he didn't immediately invite her inside.

"Of course. I didn't mean to be rude. I was writing."

"Writing?" She followed him into his living room and when he gestured toward the sofa, she sat there, hoping she appeared serene and cool. As though this was nothing more than a social call, when in fact the direction of her whole life rested on this meeting with Colby. She had too much experience in negotiating to allow her feelings to show, but she was more nervous about this visit than about any business deal she'd ever accomplished.

"I've been working on an article for the *American Journal of Medicine,*" he elaborated. "The editor asked me six months ago if I'd be willing to contribute a piece and I'm only getting around to it now."

Valerie felt a surge of pride. Colby had a wonderful future ahead of him. The world would be a better place because of his dedication and caring. Their eyes held for several moments. Valerie wanted to tell him how much she admired him, how proud she was of him, but she couldn't. She didn't want anything she said now to sway his decision later.

"I have something to ask you," she said, standing abruptly. She glanced around, then slowly sat back down again.

"Yes?" His gaze fell to her hands and she realized she was rubbing her palms together. She instantly stopped, embarrassed by this small display of nervousness.

"The last time I saw you," she began in a voice that was more hesitant than she'd intended, "when we last talked, you asked me to leave Orchard Valley."

"Yes," he admitted harshly.

"Why?"

"You know the answer to that as well as I do. Your father's recovery has amazed everyone. Eventually you're going back, so I can't see any reason to prolong this . . . interlude. Texas is where you belong."

"In other words, if a man's going to hold me and kiss me, it should be Rowdy Cassidy."

A brief flash of anger showed in his eyes, but was almost immediately quelled. "That's exactly what I mean," he returned smoothly.

"I can't help asking myself something," she said, her voice growing smaller despite her best efforts. "Is my leaving what you really want?"

"What do you mean?"

"I could stay in Orchard Valley." Her gaze clung to his, hopefully, eagerly. "This is my home. It's where I was born and raised, where I attended school. Some of my friends still live here and I know just about everyone in town." The words were rushed, crowding one another.

Colby breathed in deeply and seemed to hold his breath. His hands tightened into fists. "Why would you do that?"

Valerie had wondered how Colby would respond. She knew what she wanted him to say—that he longed for her to stay, that he needed her in his life. Instead, he'd responded with a cruelly flippant question.

"Why would I stay?" she repeated slowly, her gaze never wavering from his. "Because, Colby, you're here."

Her words were met with a brief, tension-wrought silence as though her frankness had shocked him. He looked away.

"Are you saying you love me?" he demanded in a voice that suggested this wasn't what he wanted to hear.

"Yes." The lone word was husky with something close to regret. "All morning I've been wishing I'd dated more in high school and college, because then I'd know what to say. I've always been too...forward. I can't help it. It's just part of my nature."

Colby said nothing, which made her hurry to fill the silence.

"This is when you're supposed to admit you love me too," she prompted anxiously. "That is, if you do... I may not have been a Homecoming Queen, but I'm woman enough to know you care for me, Colby Winston. The least you can do is admit it and let me salvage what little pride I have left."

"Loving you has never been the problem."

"Thank you for that," she whispered.

"It isn't enough."

"But how do we know that? We haven't even tried. It seems to me no one would have gotten anywhere in this world if they'd decided to quit before even trying."

"You make it so damn tempting."

"I do? I really do?" His words thrilled her. They gave her the first sign of encouragement since her arrival. "I was thinking... there are other companies around Oregon that I could work for... that would be glad to have me."

Colby stood and walked away from her. Not knowing what else to do, Valerie followed him.

"I think you should kiss me," she said hoarsely.

"Valerie." He turned as he said her name. He wasn't expecting her to be so close behind him because he nearly collided with her. His hands reached for her shoulders in an effort to steady her.

It was exactly what Valerie had hoped would happen. She moved automatically into his embrace, wrapping her arms around his middle, hugging him close. She raised her mouth expectantly to his and wasn't disappointed.

With a groan, Colby claimed her lips. His hands were in her hair as he tilted her head back and kissed her with a hunger that left her breathless and weak.

"Valerie...no." Reluctantly he eased away from her, bracing his hands against her shoulders.

"But why?" she pleaded.

Deftly Colby stepped back, putting as much distance between them as possible. "What's wrong with you?" he asked angrily.

"Wrong?" she repeated, still trapped in the excitement his kiss had aroused.

"Did you think coming here and seducing me would mean an offer of marriage? It's not very original, Valerie. I would have thought better of you."

"Seduce you?" Hot color instantly sprang into her cheeks. "I wasn't...I had no intention—"

"Well, that's the way it looked to me."

If he was trying to rile her, he was certainly doing an effective job. She forced herself to take several deep, calming breaths. "I didn't come here to seduce you, Colby, nor am I going to allow you to annoy me into an argument. Believe what you want. I came because I had to know. I had to find out for myself if there was a chance for us. If not, tell me so right now and I'll leave. I'll walk out that door and we'll both forget I was ever here."

He frowned, his expression fierce, but he didn't answer.

"Say it," she demanded. "Tell me you don't want me. Tell me to get out of your life and I'll go, Colby. I won't even look back."

She remained on the far side of the room, frozen in misery.

Still Colby said nothing. Nothing.

"You don't need to worry about any unpleasant scenes. I'll pack up my belongings, drive myself to the airport, and you'll never hear from me again." Her voice remained steady despite the hoarseness of pain.

He remained silent.

"Just say it," she cried. "Tell me to go . . . if that's what you want. But if you had an ounce of sense, you'd ask me to stay right here and marry you. You don't have any sense, though, do you? I know—because you're going to do what you think is the noble thing and send me away. Well, I won't make it easy for you, Colby, not this time. If you want me out of your life, you're going to have to say it."

"I might if I could get a word in edgewise."

Valerie choked on a sob and swallowed the laughter. "I love you! Doesn't that mean anything to you?"

His hands clenched into tight fists again, and his eyes, his beautiful eyes, didn't stray from her.

"Say it!" she shouted. "Tell me you don't want me. Better yet, tell me you're crazy in love with me and that you're willing to find a way to make everything right for us. Tell me that instead."

He closed his eyes.

"This is it, Colby. If I walk out that door, whatever was between us is over. I'll go about my business and you'll go about yours. I refuse to waste the rest of my life waiting for you.'' She dashed the tears from her cheeks with the back of her hand.

"You'll always be someone very special in my life." The words were so that she barely heard them.

"That's not good enough," she sobbed. "Tell me to get out of your life. Make it strong enough so I'll know you mean it, so I won't question it later. So *you* won't question it later."

"You don't belong here."

"That's better," she gulped. "But still not good enough. Haven't you ever heard of being cruel in order to be kind? Just make sure you mean what you say, because this is the only chance you'll have." Her voice broke. "You don't even have to promise to marry me. Just ask me to stay."

"No!" It was shouted at her, as though something had snapped inside him. "You want me to be cruel, is that what it takes? Does it need to come to this? You're an intelligent woman, or so I assumed, but this...this performance is ridiculous. I owe you nothing. You want me to tell you to go? Then go. You don't need my permission." He stormed to the other side of the room and held open the door for her. "Go back to Texas, Valerie. Marry your cowboy."

Stunned, she was afraid to move, afraid her legs would no longer support her. She nodded. Trembling, she moved past him.

"Goodbye," she whispered and then, unable to resist, brushed her fingertips down the side of his face. When she looked back to this moment, there would be no regrets. She'd offered him everything she had to give, and he was turning her away. There was nothing more she could do.

COLBY GLANCED at his hands, the very hands he used to save lives, and saw they were trembling with the force of an emotion so strong that it was all he could do not to smash them into a concrete wall.

When Valerie had first left, he'd been furious. He would have preferred it if she'd packed her bags and quietly disappeared. That was what he'd envisioned. Not this dreadful scene. Not dragging out their emotions like this.

He wanted to shake her for forcing him to send her away. But he was the one left trembling. It shouldn't have been so difficult. This wasn't a new decision, but one he'd made long before he'd ever kissed her, long before he'd held her in his arms and comforted her.

The phone rang and he reached for it, grateful for the reprieve from his thoughts. ''Hello,'' he snapped, not meaning to sound so impatient.

''Colby, is this a bad time?''

''Sherry...of course not. I was just thinking...'' He let the rest fade.

''I'm sorry, but I won't be able to make our dinner date tonight, after all.''

How sweet she sounded, Colby mused. Sweet and gentle. Oh, Lord, why couldn't he feel for her the things he felt for Valerie Bloomfield? Heaven knew he'd tried in the past few days. He'd done whatever he could think of to spark their interest in each other, but to no avail.

"My Aunt Janice arrived and my parents thought it would be a good idea if I took her over to my brother's place," Sherry explained. "I hope this isn't inconvenient for you."

"No problem." He heard something else in her voice, a hesitancy, a disappointment, but he chose not to question it.

"Colby."

"Yes?" The irritation was back, but it wasn't Sherry who'd angered him. It was his own lack of feeling for her. This past week, he'd spent four evenings with her. He'd held her and kissed her, and each time her kisses had left him cold and untouched.

"I don't mean to be tactless, but I don't think we should date each other anymore."

Her words shocked him. "Why not?" he demanded, although he knew the reasons and didn't blame her.

"It's not me you're interested in, it's Norah's sister. I like you, Colby, don't get me wrong, but this just isn't working. We've been seeing each other for over a year now, and if we were going to fall in love it would have happened before now."

"We haven't given it a real chance." Colby didn't understand why he was arguing with her when he was in full agreement. Sherry would make some man a wonderful wife. Some *other* man.

"You're using me, Colby."

He had nothing to say in his own defense. He hadn't realized until she'd said it, but Sherry was right. He *had* been using her. Not to make Valerie jealous, or in any devious, underhanded way, but in an effort to prove to himself that he could happily live the rest of his life without Valerie.

But the experiment had backfired. And now he was alone, wondering how he could have allowed the only woman he'd ever loved to walk out of his life.

"WHAT'S THIS I hear about you going back to Texas?" David Bloomfield asked when Valerie joined him on the front porch following the evening meal. She sat on the top step, her back pressed against the white column while her father rocked gently in his old chair. Her gaze wandered over the blooming apple orchard, the soft scent of pink and white blossoms perfuming the air. The setting sun cast a golden glow across the sky and over the land.

Valerie hadn't said anything at dinner about returning to Texas, and was surprised that her father was aware of her intention. She'd sat quietly in her place at the table, pushing the food around her plate and hoping no one would notice she wasn't eating.

"It's time for me to go back, Daddy."

"It hurts, doesn't it?" he asked, his voice tender.

"A little." *A lot,* her heart cried, but it was a cry she'd been ignoring from the moment she left Colby's home. "You're better now," she said with forced cheerfulness. "You don't need me around here any longer."

"Ah, but I do," her father countered smoothly, continuing to rock in his chair. "Colby needs you, too."

His name went through her like the blade of a sharp sword, and her breath caught at the unexpected pain.

Her father was the reason she'd come home, but Colby was the reason she was leaving.

"Love is funny, isn't it?" she mused, wrapping her arms around her knees the way she had as a young girl.

"You and I are so much alike," her father said. "Your mother saw it before I did, which I suppose is only natural. I'm proud of you, Valerie, proud of what you've managed to accomplish in so short a time, your professionalism. Cassidy's lucky to have you on his team, and he knows it, otherwise he wouldn't have promoted you."

"I've got a wonderful future with CHIPS." She said it to remind herself that her life did have purpose. There was somewhere to focus all her energy. Something that would help her forget, give her a reason to go on.

"Your mother's and my romance wasn't so easy, either, you know," her father continued, rocking slowly. "She was this pretty young nurse, and I was head over heels in love with her. To my mind, she was lucky to have me. Problem was, she didn't seem to think so. I was a millionaire. In the years since the war I'd amassed a fortune. But none of that impressed your mother." His smile was wryly nostalgic, his eyes gazing at a long ago world. "Convincing Grace to marry me was by far the most difficult task I'd faced in years."

"She didn't love you?" That seemed impossible for Valerie to comprehend.

"She loved me, all right, she just didn't think she'd make me the right kind of wife. I was wealthy, socially prominent, and your mother was a preacher's daughter. Before I contracted rheumatic fever I was one of the most sought-after bachelors in California, if I do say so myself. But I hadn't met the woman I wanted to marry until your mother became my nurse."

How achingly familiar this sounded to Valerie. She'd been content with her own life until she met Colby. Falling in love was the last thing she'd expected when she returned home.

"There were other problems, too," David went on. "Your mother seemed to think my work habits would kill me, and she wasn't willing to marry me only to watch me work myself to death."

"But you solved everything."

"Eventually." A wistful look stole over him. "I loved your mother from the first moment I opened my eyes and saw her standing beside the hospital bed. I remember thinking she was an angel, and in some ways she was." His face shone with the strength of unending love. "I knew if she'd ever agree to marry me, I was going to have to give up everything I'd worked so hard to achieve. That meant selling my business and finding something new to occupy my time."

"You did it, though."

"Not without a lot of deliberation. I'd already made more money than I knew how to spend, but I realized I wasn't going to be happy retiring before the age of forty. I had to have something to do. It took a couple of years—and Grace's help—to figure out what that should be."

Valerie nodded. "I feel the same way. I'd never be content just sitting at home— I'm too much like you." The extent of his sacrifice shook her. "How could you have given up everything you'd worked all those years to build?"

"My life without your mother would have been empty. My work didn't matter anymore. Grace was important, and the life we were going to build together was important. I gave up one life, but gained another, one that I found far more fulfilling."

"But didn't you ever get bored or restless?"

"Some, but not nearly as much as I expected. When we'd been married a year or two, your mother realized I had too much time on my hands and we looked around for something to occupy me, some interest. That was when we bought the orchard and moved here." He grinned. "My own Garden of Eden."

"I don't think I ever realized how much you'd altered your life to marry Mom."

"It was a sacrifice, and at the time it seemed like a huge one, but as the years passed, I realized she'd been right. I would have killed myself had I continued in business. Your mother brought balance into my life, the same way Colby will bring balance into yours."

She allowed a moment to pass before she spoke. "I'm not marrying Colby, Dad. I wish I could tell you I was, and that we were going to seek the same happiness you found with Mom, but it isn't going to happen."

It was as if she hadn't said a word. "You're going to be so good for him, Valerie. He loves you now, and you love him, but what you feel for each other doesn't even begin to approach the love you'll experience over the years, especially after the children arrive.''

''Dad, you're not listening to me.'' He seemed to be in a dream world that shut out reality. She had to make him stop, had to pull him out of the fantasy.

''He needs you, too, you know, even more than you need him. Colby's lived alone too many years. It's only been recently that he's recognized how much he wants a woman in his life.''

''He doesn't want me.''

Her father closed his eyes and smiled. ''You don't honestly believe that, do you? He wants you so much it's eating him alive.''

She hadn't the strength to argue with her father, not after her confrontation with Colby earlier in the day. Nor did she have the energy to explain what had passed between them. In her mind, it was finished, over. She'd told him she wouldn't look back and she meant it. She'd swallowed her pride and gone to him and he'd cast her out of his life.

She didn't hate him for being cruel; she'd asked for that. Nor had she made it easy for him to reject her. But he'd done it.

David sipped his coffee, and his smile grew even more serene. ''You have such happiness awaiting you, Valerie. This business with my heart is a good example of good coming out of bad. My attack was what brought you racing home. Heaven only knows how long it would have been before you met Colby if it weren't for this bum heart of mine.''

Valerie reached for her own mug of coffee and took a sip. ''You want anything more before I head in?''

"So soon? It's not even dark."

"I have a lot to do."

"Are you going to think about what I said?"

She hated to disappoint him, hated to disillusion a romantic old man whose judgment was clouded by thirty years of loving one woman.

"I'll think about it," Valerie promised, but it was a lie. She fully intended to push every thought, every memory of Colby completely from her mind. It was the only way she'd be able to function. She got slowly to her feet.

"Good." He nodded, still smiling. "Stay with me, then. There's no need for you to hurry inside."

Valerie hesitated. This conversation was becoming decidedly uncomfortable. She didn't want to disillusion her father, but she had to face what had happened between her and Colby, accept it as truth and get on with her life. Pining away for him would solve nothing. And listening to her father only added to the pain.

"I need to do a few things before I leave." The excuse was weak, but it was all she could think to say.

"There's plenty of time. Sit with me a spell. Relax."

"Dad . . . please."

"I want to tell you something important."

"What is it, Dad?" she asked, her voice barely a whisper.

"I know for a fact that you're going to marry Colby," he said, smiling up at her, his eyes bright and clear. "Your mother promised me."

CHAPTER NINE

"DAD," Valerie said, suppressing the urge to argue with him. "If it's about your dream, I don't think—"

"It was more than a dream! I was dead. I told you—ask Colby if you don't believe me. I crossed over into the valley of shadows. Your mother was waiting for me there and she wasn't pleased. No, sir. She was downright irritated with me. Said it wasn't my time to die yet, and I was coming home much too early."

"I'm sure this seemed very real to you—"

"It *was* real." His voice was strong. "Now you sit down and listen, because what I'm about to tell you happened as surely as I live and breathe."

Trapped, Valerie did as her father asked, lowering herself to the top porch step. "All right, Dad, I'll listen."

"Good." He smiled briefly down at her, apparently appeased. "I've missed your mother, and I didn't want to continue living in this world without her. She told me my thinking was all wrong. She promised me the years I have left will be full and happy ones, with nothing like the loneliness I've endured since she's been gone."

"Of course they will be." Valerie didn't put much stock in this near-death experience of her father's, but he believed it and that was the important thing.

"Problem was, I didn't much care about my life back here," he continued, almost as if he hadn't heard Valerie. "I was with Grace and that was where I wanted to be. As far as I was concerned I wasn't going back."

Valerie was completely familiar with her father's stubbornness; she'd inherited a streak of it herself.

"Your mother told me there was a reason for me to return. To tell you the truth, I'd already decided I wasn't going to let her talk me into it. She was darn good at that, you know. She'd drag me into the most outlandish things and make me think it was all my idea."

Her father was grinning as he spoke, his eyes twinkling with a rare joy.

"That was when she told me about you girls. Your mother and I were standing by a small lake." He frowned, apparently trying to remember each detail of his experience. "She asked me to look into the water. I thought it an unusual request, considering the seriousness of the discussion we were having."

"What did you see?" Valerie was thinking of trout and maybe some bass, knowing how much her father enjoyed lazing away a summer's afternoon fishing.

"I saw the future."

"The future?" This sounded like something out of a science-fiction novel.

"You heard me," he said irritably. "The water was like a window and I was able to look into years ahead.

I saw you and your sisters, and you know what? It was the most beautiful scene I could ever have imagined. So much joy, so much laughter and love. I couldn't stop looking, couldn't stop smiling. There were my precious daughters, all so happy, all so blessed with love, the same way your mother and I had been."

"It sounds lovely, Dad." Her father had undergone traumatic surgery and just barely survived. If he believed in this dream, if he maintained he'd actually spoken to her mother, then Valerie couldn't bring herself to disillusion him with reality. Nor did she want to argue with him. Especially not now, when her own heart had taken such a beating.

"I remember every single moment of that meeting with your mother. You know, I didn't see a single angel. I don't mind telling you, that was a bit of a disappointment. Nor did I hear anyone playing the harp."

Valerie suppressed a smile.

"You understand what I'm saying, don't you?"

"About angels?"

"No," he returned impatiently. "About you and Colby. He's the one I saw you with, Val. You had three beautiful children."

"Dad, why now?" At his quizzical gaze, she elaborated. "Why are you trying so hard to convince me to marry Colby? After the surgery, you seemed to have given up the idea. What happened to change your mind?"

"You did."

"Me?"

"You're both so darned stubborn. I hadn't counted on that."

"But you apologized for the matchmaking, remember?"

"Of course I remember. I did give it up on Grace's advice, but only because I felt you two wouldn't need any help from me. But I quickly found out you need my help more than ever. That's why I talked about Cassidy so much. To get you thinking about what you really wanted. And to make Colby a little jealous. Face it, Val. Eventually you're going to marry him—there's no doubt of it."

"Dad, please, I know you want to believe this, but it just isn't going to happen." Without realizing what he was doing, her own father was making everything so much more painful.

"Don't you understand, child? Colby loves you, and you love him, and you're going to have a wonderful life together. Naturally there'll be ups and downs, but there are in any marriage."

"I'm not marrying Colby," she said between gritted teeth.

"You think I'm an old man whose elevator doesn't go all the way to the top, but you're wrong." He gave her a lazy smile. "I know what I saw. All I'm asking is that you be patient with Colby and patient with yourself. Just don't do anything foolish."

"Like what?"

"Returning to Texas. You belong here in Orchard Valley now. It's where you're going to raise your children and where Colby's going to continue his practice."

"It's too late."

"For what?"

Valerie stood, her chest aching with the effort to breathe normally. She felt so empty, so alone. More than anything, she wanted to believe her father's dream, but she couldn't. She just couldn't.

"I've already booked my flight. I leave in the morning." She didn't wait for her father to argue with her, to tell her what a terrible mistake she was making. Instead she hurried into the house and up the stairs, not stopping until she was inside her room, with the door firmly closed.

She hauled her suitcase from the closet. There wasn't much to pack, and the entire process took her all of five minutes. She didn't weep. Her tears had already been spent.

When she returned to Texas, she'd be more mindful of love. It had touched her life once; perhaps it would again. In time. When her heart had healed. When she was ready.

With that thought in mind, she reached for the phone on the nightstand and held it in her lap, staring sightlessly at the numbers. After an endless moment, she tapped out the long-distance number.

"Hello." The deep male voice sounded hurried and impatient.

"Hello, Rowdy," she said quietly.

"Valerie." He seemed delighted to be hearing from her. "I'm glad you phoned. I tried to reach you earlier in the day, but your sister told me you were out. I don't suppose she happened to mention my call?"

"No. Was it something important?" It could only have been Norah, since Steffie was out most of the day. Romantic Norah, who wanted so badly for Valerie to marry Colby and live happily ever after.

"It wasn't urgent. I just wanted to see how soon CHIPS could have you back. There's been a big hole here since you left."

"I realize my being gone has been an inconvenience—"

"Don't be silly. I wasn't referring to the workload, I was talking about *you*. Like I told you before, I sort of got used to having you around," he said gruffly, as though he was uncomfortable saying such things. "It doesn't seem right with you not here. You're an important part of my team. That's how come I'm giving you a ten percent raise—just so you'll know how much you're appreciated."

Valerie gasped. "That isn't necessary."

"Sure it is. Now, when are you flying home?"

Home. It wasn't in Texas, it never really had been, but Rowdy wouldn't understand that.

"Valerie?"

"Oh, sorry. That was actually the reason for my call. I've booked my flight for tomorrow morning. I'll arrive early in the evening and be at the office bright and early Monday morning." She forced some enthusiasm into her words.

"That's great news. It's just what I was hoping to hear. We'll celebrate. How about if I pick you up at the airport and take you to dinner?"

The invitation took her by surprise, although she supposed it shouldn't have. "Ah…" She didn't know what to say. She'd already promised herself she wasn't going to pine away the rest of her life for Colby Winston. Yet when the opportunity arose to place the past firmly behind her and begin a new life, she hesitated.

"I don't think so," she told him regretfully. "Not just yet. I'm going to need some time to readjust after being away for so long." It had been less than three weeks, but it felt like a whole lifetime.

"You've been gone too long," Rowdy said, his voice low and resonant. "I've missed you, Valerie. I haven't made a secret of it, either. When you get back, I'd like it if the two of us could sit down and talk."

Sudden dread attacked her stomach, her nerves. This wasn't what she wanted to hear. "I—I don't know if that'd be a good idea, Rowdy. I don't mean to be—"

"I know what you're thinking," Rowdy cut in. "And I have to admit, I share your concern. An office romance can lead to problems. That's why I want us to talk. Clear the air before we get involved."

It didn't seem to occur to Rowdy that she might be unwilling to date him. But not so long ago, the prospect of a relationship with him would have filled her with excitement.

RARELY HAD Colby spent a more uncomfortable night. He hadn't been able to sleep and, finally giving up, had gone downstairs to read. Another hour ticked slowly by, and still his mind refused to relax. Feeling even more disgruntled, he set the novel aside.

It would have helped if Sherry had kept her dinner date, but she'd cancelled. Not only that, but she'd let him know she didn't want to see him again. She was right to have done it, too—a fact that didn't improve his disposition.

When it came to his relationships with women, Colby just wasn't getting anywhere. Okay, so he was behind schedule. He'd underestimated the difficulty in finding the type of wife he wanted. That was understandable.

His requirements were very specific, which was why he'd intended to conduct his search in a methodical, orderly manner. It wasn't as though he'd discovered any shortage of "old-fashioned" girls, either. It just so happened that most of them didn't appeal to him.

This realization only served to confuse him further. Obviously there was some kind of flaw in his plan. Of one thing he was certain—Sherry was out of the picture. For that matter, so was Valerie.

Valerie.

Her name burned his mind, and by sheer force of will, he turned his thoughts in another direction. He got up and moved into his den for the printout of the article he'd been working on earlier that day. Although he'd shrugged off the importance of this article when he spoke to Valerie, he was well aware that the invitation to submit it was a real honor. He'd done exhaustive research, and every word he'd written had been carefully considered.

But right then and there, Colby realized it meant nothing. Nothing. With an angry burst of energy, he crumpled the sheets and tossed them into his wastebasket.

Colby rarely acted in anger. Rarely did he allow himself to display any emotion. He'd schooled himself well; he'd needed to. He dealt with death so often, with fear, with grief. It became crucial, a matter of emotional survival, to keep his own feelings strictly private. Over the years, it had become second nature. For the first time in recent memory, he regretted his inexperience at expressing emotion.

He had no trouble recognizing that his inability to sleep, his lack of interest in a good novel, his discontent with the article he was writing, were all wrapped up in what had happened between him and Valerie that morning.

He'd done what he had to do. It hadn't been easy—for either of them—but it was necessary. She'd made him angry, he realized, with her demand that he be cruel. She wouldn't accept anything less. By the time she left, he'd been furious. She'd prodded and pushed and shoved until, backed into a corner, he'd had no choice.

Every harsh word he'd spoken had boomeranged back to hit him. She'd insisted repeatedly that he tell her to get out of his life. And he'd done it....

It was over, which was exactly what he wanted. Valerie would go back to Texas and he'd continue living here in Orchard Valley.

Her eyes would haunt him, he decided next, rubbing his face with a weary hand. They'd been gray and sad, and it had taken the better part of the afternoon to forget the feel of her fingertips as they grazed his face.

His intention had been to send her away, hurt her if he had to, so the break would be final. What took him by surprise was how much it had cost him.

Twenty hours later, and he was still angry. He still hurt.

Walking back into his living room, Colby sank into the recliner and reached for the television remote control. It was early morning; surely there'd be some movie playing that would hold his attention for an hour or two.

He was wrong. The only show he could find was a 1950s love story, filmed in nostalgic black and white. The last thing Colby was in the mood to watch was a sentimental romance with a happy ending. He turned off the television and stood up.

It had been three days since he'd been out to the Bloomfields'. Although David was home and they'd scheduled an appointment at the office early in the week, it wouldn't be a bad idea to stop in and see how the older man was recovering. They were friends, and it was the least Colby could do—for the sake of a longstanding friendship.

With that decision made, he found himself yawning loudly. Fatigue greeted him like an old comrade, and in that moment Colby knew he'd be able to sleep.

VALERIE WAS DRESSED, her suitcase packed. She'd lingered in her room far longer than necessary. Her flight wasn't scheduled until 1:00 p.m.—not for another four hours—so she had plenty of time, yet she felt a burning need to be on her way. But there was another feeling that ran even deeper, even stronger: she dreaded leaving.

"Valerie?"

She turned to find Steffie standing in her bedroom doorway, frowning as her gaze fell on the suitcase. "Are you sure you're doing the right thing?"

Valerie gave her a wide and completely artificial smile. "I'm positive."

"How can you smile?"

"It's such a beautiful morning, how could I possibly be sad? Dad's home and thriving, you're here, and Norah's in seventh heaven because she's got someone to cook for."

Steffie grinned. "Yeah, I know. But I can't help feeling you shouldn't go."

"My life's in Texas now."

Steffie strolled into the room and sat on the end of the bed. "If you're running away, it's a mistake. I made the same one myself three years ago. I made an idiot of myself over Charles Tomaselli, and then because I was so embarrassed and because I couldn't bear to face him again, I decided to study in Europe."

"You had a wonderful opportunity to travel. Do you honestly regret it?"

"Yes. Oh, not the travel and the experience. But my leaving was wrong. I didn't realize it then, but I do now. I went into hiding. I know that sounds melodramatic, but it's the truth. At the time it seemed like the only thing to do, but I realize now I should have swallowed my pride instead of walking away from everything I loved."

"Sometimes we don't have any choice."

"And sometimes we do," Steffie countered softly. "Don't make the same mistake I did. Don't run away, because at some point down the road, you're going to regret it, just like I did."

Her sister's eyes were intent, silently pleading with Valerie to reconsider. If she hadn't gone to Colby the day before, Valerie might have hesitated, but there was no reason now for her to stay. There was no reason to hope Colby would change his mind.

"Someone's coming," Steffie said, wandering over to look out Valerie's bedroom window.

Valerie moved aside the white curtains and glanced outside. Steffie was right. A maroon car was making its way down the long driveway.

Colby.

A surge of excitement shot through her. He'd come to tell her he'd changed his mind, to ask her not to leave. Only seconds before, she'd been so certain there was no hope and now it flowed through her like current into an electrical wire. Try as she might, she couldn't squelch it.

"It—it's Colby," Valerie said, when she found her voice.

Steffie let out a cry of sheer joy. "I knew it. I knew he wasn't going to be able to let you go. It didn't make sense. Everyone knows the way he feels about you, the way you feel about him. He'd be a fool if he let you go back to Texas."

"He didn't know I was leaving this morning," Valerie said calmly, though he must have figured it out for himself. She wouldn't stay in Orchard Valley any longer than necessary, and they both recognized that.

"I'll find out what he wants," Steffie said, her voice high and excited. "Let's play this cool, okay? You stay up here and when he asks to see you, I'll casually come get you."

"Steffie..."

"Valerie, for heaven's sake, be romantic for once in your life."

"There could be plenty of other reasons Colby's here."

"Are you going to make him suffer, or are you going to forgive him right away? Personally, I think he should suffer... but only a little."

The doorbell chimed and Steffie hurried downstairs without another word.

Valerie couldn't keep her heart from racing, but she refused to play this silly game of wait-and-see. She reached for her suitcase and started resolutely down the stairs, the way she'd originally intended.

She was on the top step when she heard Colby ask to see her father. *Her father—not her.* If it hadn't hurt so much, Valerie would have laughed at Steffie, who looked completely stunned. Her sister stared at Colby, her mouth dangling open, hand frozen on the door, blocking his entrance.

"My father," Steffie repeated after a shocked moment. "You're here to see Dad?"

"He is my patient."

"I know, but..."

Some slight, telltale sound must have alerted Colby that Valerie was standing at the top of the stairs. His gaze rose and linked with hers before slowly lowering to the suitcase in her hand. Valerie detected a slight frown, as though he'd been caught by surprise.

"Valerie's leaving this morning," Steffie announced in a loud, urgent voice as though Colby had better do something fast.

What Steffie hadn't grasped was that Colby didn't intend to do anything—other than bid her a relieved farewell.

"You might want to tell Dad Dr. Winston's here," Valerie said mildly. "He's probably in the kitchen."

Steffie left, and Valerie gradually descended the stairs.

"Looks like you're packed up and ready to go," he said in a conversational tone.

She nodded. "My flight leaves at one."

"So soon?"

"Not soon enough, though, is it, Colby?"

He ignored the question, and Valerie regretted the pettiness that had prompted her to ask. He stood before her, his expression unreadable. She was grateful when her father appeared. Grateful because she wasn't nearly as expert at hiding her feelings as Colby. She feared he could read much more of her emotional turmoil than she wanted him to.

"Colby, my boy, it's good to see you. You've been making yourself scarce the last few days." David steered Colby into the kitchen, then glanced back at Valerie, scowling at the suitcase in her hand. "You've got plenty of time, Val. Come and have a cup of coffee before you leave."

For her father's sake, she resisted the temptation to argue. Shrugging, she set her luggage aside and dutifully followed Colby and David into the large family kitchen.

The two men sat at the table while Norah served them coffee. Valerie didn't sit with the others, but pulled out a stool in front of the counter and perched on that.

"I thought I'd check in and see how you were feeling," Colby was saying.

"Never felt better," her father replied.

Valerie noticed how Colby avoided glancing in her direction. He was uncomfortable with her; his back was stiff, his shoulders rigid with tension. Perhaps he'd expected her to have left by now.

Valerie sipped her coffee and briefly closed her eyes, wanting to savor these last few moments with her family. Norah, an apron tied around her waist, was busily pulling hot cinnamon rolls from the oven. Homemade ones, from the recipe their mother had used through the years. The scent of yeast and spice filled the kitchen, and it was like stepping back in time. Their kitchen had always been where everyone gathered, a place of warmth and laughter and confidences shared.

Steffie couldn't seem to stand still. She paced to one side of the room, then crossed to the other, as though debating her next course of action.

Valerie found it endearing that her sister cared so much about what happened between her and Colby, especially when Steffie's own romance continued to be so trying. Valerie sensed that things weren't going well between her sister and Charles Tomaselli, but she wasn't in any position to be offering advice.

Steffie paused, her eyes pleading with Valerie. She seemed to be begging her to reconsider. To stay in Orchard Valley, to listen to her heart ...

After a moment Valerie couldn't meet her sister's gaze and purposely looked away.

Conversation floated past her, but she wasn't aware of what was being said or who was saying it. The sudden need to leave was too strong to ignore. If she didn't do it soon, she might never be able to go. Slipping down from the stool, she deposited her mug, still half full of coffee, in the sink.

"The rolls will be ready to eat any moment," Norah said, looking at her anxiously. She, too, seemed to want Valerie to linger.

"Don't worry, I'll pick up something to eat at the airport later."

"Are you leaving?" her father asked, as if this was a surprise to him. "You've still got lots of time."

Valerie offered the first excuse that came to mind. "I've got to get the rental car back to the agency."

"You're *sure* you want to go?" Steffie asked forlornly, moving toward her sister.

"I'm sure," Valerie answered in a soft voice, giving Steffie an affectionate hug. "It isn't like I'll never be back, you know?"

"Don't let it take you three years, the way it did me," Steffie whispered close to Valerie's ear. "I just can't help thinking you're making a mistake."

"It's for the best," Valerie said.

Norah stood behind Steffie, waiting her turn to be hugged, her pretty blue eyes as sad as Steffie's. "I can't believe you're really going. It's been so good having you home."

"It's been fun, hasn't it, Dad?" Valerie said, trying to lighten the atmosphere. "I'd like to suggest another family reunion, only next time let's plan things a bit differently. If I'm going to take another three weeks away from CHIPS, I'd prefer to see more than a hospital waiting room."

David Bloomfield stood, his gaze holding Valerie's. He seemed to be asking her to remain a few minutes longer, but she firmly shook her head. Every moment was torture.

She dared not look in Colby's direction. That made it easier to pretend he wasn't there.

"I have a great idea for a family reunion," Steffie suggested eagerly. "Why don't we all take a trip to Egypt? I've always wanted to ride a camel and tour the pyramids."

"Egypt?" Norah echoed. "What's wrong with a camping trip? We used to do that years ago, and it was always fun. I can remember us sitting around the camp fire singing and toasting marshmallows."

"Camping!" Steffie cried. "You can't be serious. I remember mosquitoes the size of Alabama."

"But we had fun," Norah reminded them.

"Maybe you did, but count me out," Valerie said, laughing quickly. "My idea of roughing it is going without room service." She glanced from one sister to the other, loving them both so much that her heart felt it would burst. She stepped forward and threw her arms around her father's neck.

"Take care of yourself," she whispered.

"The dream," he returned, his eyes bright and intense. "I was so sure."

Valerie didn't need to be reminded of her father's dream. "Maybe someday it'll happen." But she didn't believe it, any more than she believed the dead could come back to life.

"You're going to say goodbye to Colby, aren't you?" her father urged.

She'd been hoping to avoid it. But she recognized that it would be impossible to leave without saying something to Colby, who was her father's doctor, her father's guest. David released her and she saw that Colby was on his feet and moving toward her. It would have salvaged her pride just a little if he'd revealed at least a hint of regret. But from all outward appearances it was as if she was nothing more to him than a passing acquaintance. As if he'd never held her in his arms, never kissed her.

"Goodbye, Colby," she said as cheerfully as she could manage. "Thank you for everything you did for Dad—for all of us. You were . . . wonderful." She extended her hand, which he took in his own. His fingers tightened on hers, his grip almost painful.

"Goodbye, Valerie," he said after a moment. As before, it was impossible to read his expression. "Have a safe trip."

She nodded and turned away, afraid that if she didn't leave soon, she'd do something utterly stupid, like break down and weep.

Everyone followed her to the front porch. Eager to get away now, Valerie hurried down the stairs. Not bothering to open the trunk, she set her lone suitcase on the back seat.

"Phone once in a while, won't you?" Steffie called.

Valerie nodded. "Take care of Dad, you two."

"Bye, Val." Norah pressed her fingers to her lips.

Rather than endure another round of farewells, Valerie slid into the driver's seat and closed the door. She didn't look toward the porch for fear her eyes would meet Colby's.

Escaping was what mattered. Fleeing before she made a fool of herself a second time over a man who didn't want her.

She started the car, raised her hand in a brisk wave and pulled away. The tightness in her chest was so painful it was almost unbearable. For a moment she didn't know if she'd be able to continue. The thought that she needed a doctor was what dispersed the horrible pain. It escaped on a bubble of hysterical laughter.

She needed a doctor, all right, *a heart doctor.* With the sound of her amusement still echoing in her ears, Valerie looked back one last time, her gaze seeking out Colby's.

It cost her everything, but she managed a slow smile, a smile of gratitude for what they'd shared.

She drove away then, and she didn't glance back.

Not even once.

CHAPTER TEN

FOR LONG MINUTES, no one said a word. Colby remained frozen on the Bloomfield porch, his gaze following Valerie's rental car as it sped down the driveway. His hands knotted into tight fists at his sides, and his chest throbbed with suppressed emotion.

The timing of this visit couldn't have been worse. He'd had no idea Valerie was leaving that morning, and like a fool he'd stumbled upon the scene. He cursed himself now for not calling first.

He didn't know what he'd been thinking when he'd decided to come here. Visiting David had been an excuse. He'd come to see Valerie. He'd hoped, perhaps, to find a free moment to talk to her. But for the life of him, he didn't know what he'd intended to say. He certainly hadn't changed his mind, hadn't decided to sweep everything under the proverbial rug and pretend that love would conquer all. He'd save that kind of idealism for the world's romantics. He wasn't one of them; he was a physician and he dealt with the real world. He had no intention of deluding himself into believing they had a chance together, even if she did entertain such thoughts herself.

"I can't believe this," Stephanie cried, glaring at Colby. Tears had misted her eyes, he noted with surprise. He'd always considered weeping females cause for alarm. He never knew what to say to them.

But there'd been that time with Valerie, the night of David's surgery, Colby reminded himself. She'd been sobbing out her grief and fear. With anyone else he would have sought another family member to offer the needed consolation. But he hadn't looked for Norah that night. Instead he'd gone to Valerie himself. At first, he felt a terrible loss. He couldn't hold out hope for her father's recovery, not when everything indicated that David probably wouldn't survive the night. And so he'd sat on the concrete bench beside her and placed his arm around her shoulders.

Valerie had turned to him then, and buried her face against him. The surge of love he'd experienced in that moment was unlike anything he'd ever felt. Stroking her hair, he'd savored the feel of her in his arms.

"She'll be back," David said, interrupting Colby's memories.

"No," Stephanie argued in a trembling voice. "She won't. Not for a very long time."

"Valerie's not like that," Norah said. "She'll visit again. Soon."

"Why should she, when everything she equates with home means pain? It's too easy to stay away, too easy to make excuses and be satisfied with a phone call now and again." It sounded as though Stephanie was speaking from experience, and Colby studied David Bloomfield's second daughter.

She must have felt his scrutiny because she turned suddenly, undisguised anger flashing from her deep brown eyes.

"You might be a wonderful surgeon," she said, her gaze as hard as flint, "but you're one of the biggest fools I've ever met."

Colby blinked in surprise, but before he had a chance to respond, Stephanie ran back inside the house. Amazed at the verbal attack, he looked at Norah. They'd worked together for a number of months and he'd always been fond of her.

"I couldn't agree with my sister more," Norah said with an uncharacteristic display of temper. "You're an idiot." Having said that, she stormed into the house as well.

David chuckled, and Colby relaxed. At least one member of this family could appreciate the wisdom of his sacrifice. Stephanie and Norah acted as if he should be arrested. Both seemed to think it'd been easy for him to let Valerie drive away when nothing was further from the truth. Even now he needed to grip hold of the railing to keep from racing after her.

If only she hadn't turned at the last moment and looked straight at him. And smiled. The sweetest, most beautiful smile he'd ever seen in his life. A smile that would haunt him to his grave.

"I love her," Colby whispered, his eyes never leaving the driveway, although Valerie's car was long out of view. By now she was probably two miles down the road.

"I know," David assured him.

Something in the older man's tone caused Colby to glance at him. The inflection seemed to suggest that Colby might love Valerie but he didn't love her enough. Heaven help him, he did! He loved her so much that he'd sent her out of his life. No one, not even David Bloomfield, could fully appreciate the extent of his sacrifice.

"Rowdy Cassidy will be a much better husband for her than I ever would," Colby said, steeling himself against the pain his own words produced.

"Maybe, but I doubt it," David stated, walking over to his wicker rocking chair and easing himself into it. "I don't suppose you've noticed, but Valerie and I are a lot alike."

Colby grinned. The similarity hadn't exactly escaped him. Here were two people who each possessed a streak of stubbornness that was wider than the Mississippi. Both were intelligent, intuitive and ambitious. Hardworking. Single-minded.

"She'd never be happy living here in Orchard Valley," Colby said, his gaze returning to the driveway. He couldn't seem to make himself look away. It was as if that long narrow road was his only remaining connection with Valerie.

"You're right, of course. Valerie would never be content in a small town again. Not after living in Houston."

The reassurance should have eased the ache in his heart, but it didn't. He told himself there was no reason to linger. Carrying on a polite conversation was beyond him yet he didn't seem to have the energy to leave.

"Did I ever tell you how I met Grace?"

"I believe you did." Valerie must be three or four miles down the road by now, Colby estimated.

"Our courtship was a bit unusual. It isn't every day a man woos a woman from a hospital bed."

Colby nodded. Before long, Valerie would be close to the interstate, and then it would be impossible to catch her. *Not* that he intended to chase after her.

"Grace wasn't keen on marrying me, for a number of reasons. All good ones, I might add. She loved me, that much I knew, but to her mind love wasn't enough."

David's words diverted Colby's attention from the road. He swiveled his gaze to the older man, who was rocking contentedly as though they were discussing something as mundane as the best bait for local trout. He didn't understand.

"Grace was right. Sometimes love isn't enough," David added.

"In your case she was wrong," Colby mumbled, displeased. For the first time he understood where this discussion was leading. Valerie's father was going to force him to admit that he was as big a fool as Stephanie and Norah had claimed. Though he might be more subtle about it.

"Not really. I knew I'd need to make some real changes before Grace would agree to marry me, but I was willing to make them because I knew something she didn't."

"What was that?"

A wistful look came over David, and his eyes grew hazy. "Deep in my soul, I knew I'd never love an-

other woman the way I loved Grace. Deep in my soul,
I recognized that she was the one chance I had in this
life for real happiness. I could have done the noble
thing and left her to marry some nice young man.
There were plenty who would have thanked me for the
opportunity.''

"I see."

"I have to tell you, though, it was the most difficult decision of my life. Marrying Grace was the biggest risk I ever took, but I never regretted it. Not
once.''

Colby nodded. David was telling him exactly what
he wanted to hear. He, too, had made his decision, and
had set Valerie free to find what happiness she could.
Rowdy Cassidy was waiting in the wings, eager to fill
his place. Eager to help her forget.

Colby's mind flashed to Sherry Waterman. He liked
her and enjoyed her company. He felt the same about
Norah. But it was Valerie who set his heart on fire.
Valerie who challenged him. Valerie whom he needed.
Not anyone else, only Valerie.

"Don't you worry about her," David continued.
"She'll be fine. In time, she'll regroup and be a better
person for having experienced love. As for her marrying Rowdy Cassidy, I don't think you need concern
yourself with that, either."

"Why not?"

"Because I know my daughter. I know exactly what
I would have done had Grace decided against marrying me. I'd have gone back to my world, worked hard
and made a decent life for myself. But I would never

have fallen in love again. I wouldn't have allowed it to happen."

Colby said nothing. By now, Valerie was on the interstate. It was too late. Even if he did go after her, they wouldn't be able to stop. Not on the freeway with cars screaming past. It would be reckless and dangerous and beyond all stupidity to chase her now. Besides, what could he possibly have to say that hadn't already been said?

David stood. "You want another cup of coffee?"

"No, thanks. I should be on my way."

"I'll be in your office bright and early Tuesday morning, then."

Colby nodded. It was time to get back to his life, the life he'd had before he met Valerie Bloomfield.

VALERIE REFUSED TO CRY. She'd never been prone to tears. Even as a child, she'd hated crying, hated the way the salty tears had felt against her face.

What surprised her was how much it hurt to hold everything inside. It felt as though someone had crammed a fist down her throat and asked her to breathe normally.

In an effort to push aside the pain of leaving Colby, she focused her thoughts on all the good he'd brought into her life. Without him, she would have lost her father. Norah had admitted as much that first evening. It had been Colby who'd convinced her father to go to the hospital. It had been Colby who'd performed the life-saving surgery.

If for nothing else than her father's life, she owed him more than anyone could possibly repay.

But that wasn't all he'd given her. Dr. Colby Winston had taught her about herself, about love, about sacrifice.

She would always love him for that. Now she had to teach herself to release him, to let him go. Finding love and then freely relinquishing it might well prove to be a tricky business. She'd never given her heart to a man before. Loving Colby was the easy part. It felt as though she'd always known and loved him, as if he'd always been a part of her life. It seemed impossible that they'd met only a few weeks ago.

Leaving him was the hardest thing she'd ever done.

The self-doubts, the what-ifs and might-have-beens rolled in like giant waves, swamping her with grief and dread.

Dragging in a deep breath, she fought the urge to turn the car around and head back. Back to Orchard Valley. Back home.

Back to Colby.

Instead, she exhaled, tried to relax, tried to convince herself that everything would feel much better once she was back in Texas. She'd be able to submerge the pain in her job. When she resumed her position with CHIPS, she could begin to forget Colby and at the same time treasure the memories she had of him.

Valerie didn't realize there were tears in her eyes until she noticed how blurry the road in front of her had become. Hoping to distract herself, she turned on the radio and started humming along with a country-western singer lamenting her lost love.

"You idiot," Valerie muttered, weeping harder than ever. Irritably, she snapped off the radio. "Damn." She swiped at the tears with the back of one hand, telling herself she was too strong, too independent, for such weak emotional behavior.

It wasn't until she was changing lanes on the freeway that she noticed the Buick behind her. A maroon Buick. It was traveling at high speed, passing cars, going well above the limit.

Colby? It couldn't be.

More than likely it was just a car that looked like his. It couldn't be him. He'd never come after her. It wasn't his style. No, if he ever had a change of heart, something she didn't count on, it wouldn't be for weeks, months. Colby wasn't impulsive.

The Buick slowed down and moved directly behind Valerie's car and followed her for a moment before putting on the turn signal. If it hadn't been for the tears in her eyes she would have been able to make out the driver's features.

The car honked irritably. It *had* to be Colby. He didn't honestly expect her to stop on the freeway, did he? It wouldn't be safe. There was an exit ramp only a few miles down the road and she drove toward that, turned off when she could and parked. Luckily traffic was light, and the shoulders on both sides of the road were wide enough for her to park safely. When she eased to a stop, Colby pulled in behind her.

She'd barely had time to unfasten her seat belt before he jerked open her door.

"What are you doing here?" she demanded.

"What does it look like? I'm chasing after you."

Legs trembling, she climbed out of her car, and stood leaning against it, her hands on her hips. "This better be good, Winston. I've got a plane to catch."

"You've been crying."

"There's something in my eye."

"Both eyes apparently."

"All right, both eyes." She didn't know what silly game he thought he was playing, but she didn't have the patience for it. "Why are you here? Surely there's a reason you came racing after me."

"There's a reason."

"Good." She crossed her arms and shifted her position. Whatever Colby wanted to say was obviously causing him trouble, because he started pacing in front of her, hands clenched.

"This is even harder than I expected," he finally admitted.

Not daring to hope, Valerie said nothing.

"I can't believe what a mess I've made of this. Listen," he said, turning to face her, his expression as closed as always. "I want you to come back to Orchard Valley."

"Why?"

"Because I love you and because I'd like us to talk this through. You love me, too, Valerie. I don't think I appreciated how much until just now. It must have been so hard to come to me, to lay your heart out like that and then have me send you away. I—"

"You don't need to apologize," she broke in.

"I do."

Valerie had no idea, not the slightest, where all this was leading. She took a deep breath. "All right, you've apologized."

"Will you come back?"

"If you want to talk, we can do it at the airport." It seemed like a fair suggestion.

"I want to do more than talk," he said from between gritted teeth. "I want you to show me how we're going to make this marriage work, because damned if I know. We haven't got one thing working in our favor. Not one thing."

"Then why try?"

"Because if you leave now I'm going to regret it for the rest of my life. Sure as anything, I'm going to think back to this moment for the next fifty years and wish I'd never let you go. The problem is, I'm not sure what to do now—you've got me so tied up in knots I can't even think clearly anymore."

"You don't look happy about it."

"You're right, I'm not happy. I'm downright furious."

Valerie grinned. "Love *is* rather frightening, isn't it?"

Colby grinned, too, for the first time. "But you know something? It's living without your love that frightens me."

"Oh, Colby..."

"Let's say we did get married," he said, the gravel under his feet crunching as he paced in front of her.

"All right, let's say we did."

"Are you going to want a job outside the home?"

"Yes, Colby, I will."

"What about children?"

"Oh, yes, at least two." She found it astonishing that they should be discussing something so personal, standing at the side of a road.

"How do you propose to be both a mother and an executive?"

"How do you intend to be both a father and a surgeon? Not to mention a husband? You have a career, too, Colby."

"You can't have it all, Valerie."

"Neither can you! Besides, it doesn't have to be either or. Half the women in America maintain a career *and* a family, but there have to be compromises along the way. You're right, I won't be able to do everything alone. I couldn't even begin to try."

"I don't like the idea of farming our children out to strangers."

"Frankly, I don't, either, but there are ways of working around that, too. Ways of making the situation acceptable to both of us. For one thing, I could set up an office at home. It's not unheard of, especially these days with computers and faxes and everything. Rowdy might be willing to start a branch of the company on the West Coast, and I think he might be persuaded to pick Oregon—especially if a hard-working executive chooses to live there."

Colby nodded and thrust his hands into his pockets.

"I know I'm not what you want in a wife, Colby. You'd rather I was the kind of woman who'd be content to stay home and do needlepoint, and put up preserves. But that isn't who I am, and I can't change. I'd give anything to be the woman you want, but if I'm not true to myself, the marriage would be doomed before we even said our vows.''

''I don't think we should be concerning ourselves with some unrealistic image I've invented. What about the man *you* want?''

She smiled, and looked away. ''You're the only man I've ever wanted.''

He reached for her then, wrapping his arms tightly around her, dropping a gentle kiss on the side of her neck. A deep shudder went through him as he exhaled.

''I'm never going to be able to stop loving you.''

''Is that so terrible?'' she asked in a whisper, her throat raw.

''No, it's the most wonderful blessing of my life.'' His eyes were warm and possessive as he brought his hands up to clasp her shoulders. ''I've been arrogant and selfish. I nearly destroyed both our lives because I refused to accept the gift you offered me.''

''Oh, Colby.''

''There won't be any guarantees.''

''If I wanted guarantees, I'd buy myself a new car. Everything in life is a risk, but I've never been more willing to take one than with you.''

''I'd say we're in for an adventure.''

''Yes, but it'll be the grandest adventure of our lives.'' Her arms went around his neck as he lowered his mouth to hers. One kiss wiped out the pain and the torment of these past few days. Colby must have felt it, too, because he kissed her again and again, their need for one another insatiable, their joy boundless.

A car driving past honked noisily, disturbing them.

Valerie reluctantly broke off their kiss. "You might have chosen someplace a bit more private to propose, Dr. Winston."

"Shall we try this again later with champagne and a diamond ring?"

Valerie nodded because speaking when her heart was so full would have been difficult.

HER FATHER was sitting on the porch when Valerie and Colby pulled up in front of the house late that afternoon.

"Did you tell Dad you were coming after me?"

"I didn't know it myself until I left here. Before I realized what I was doing, I was on the freeway, racing after you like a bat out of hell. I hadn't a clue what I was going to say when I found you."

Valerie tucked her hand in his and pressed her cheek to his shoulder. "You looked like you wanted to bite my head off."

"I looked like a man who was calling himself every kind of fool in existence."

"For coming after me?"

"No," he said quietly. "For letting you go."

Valerie rewarded him with an appreciative kiss on the corner of his mouth.

Colby groaned softly. "I'm not going to want a long engagement. The sooner we can arrange this wedding, the better."

"I couldn't agree more."

Colby kissed her lightly on the lips. "I have the sneaking suspicion your father hasn't moved since you left for the airport."

They'd been gone for hours, returning the rental car to Portland, and then stopping for an elegant lunch in an equally elegant restaurant. Before leaving the city, they'd visited a well-known jewelry store where Valerie chose a beautiful solitaire diamond engagement ring. That very ring was on her finger now. It felt as if it had always been there.

"About time you two were getting back," her father said as Colby helped her out of his car. "I was beginning to worry."

"How'd you know we were coming?" Colby asked.

"I knew before you left here that you'd be back with Valerie before the end of the day."

"Dad, you couldn't possibly have known." She waited for a protest, but none came. Her father sat back down in his rocker and grinned knowingly.

"Oh, I know more than that about what's going to happen to you two."

"He's going to start talking about that dream again," Valerie murmured, slipping her arm around Colby's waist and smiling up at him. He brought her close to his side.

"Love's shocked you both," David said, wagging a finger at them. "But there are a few more shocks in store for you. Just you wait and see what happens when my twin grandsons are born."

"Twins?" Colby echoed incredulously.

"You're going to name them after their two grand-fathers. The blond one will be David, and he'll be the spitting image of me."

"Twins," Colby said again.

"I don't know," Valerie said with a soft laugh. "I could get used to a few surprises now and again, especially if it means I can be with you."

Colby gazed down at her and Valerie realized her father was right. Love had caught them unawares, but it was the best surprise of their lives.

* * * * *

*Next month, join Valerie's sister, Stephanie—
the middle Bloomfield daughter—as she
resumes her tempestuous romance with the
unpredictable Charles Tomaselli. Stephanie has
to confront not only her past actions but the
future course of her life. And then there's that
dream of her father's . . .*
STEPHANIE, *Book 2 of Debbie Macomber's
Orchard Valley trilogy.
Harlequin Romance #3239.*

HARLEQUIN ROMANCE®

**Harlequin Romance
has love in
store for you!**

Don't miss next
month's title in

THE BRIDAL COLLECTION

A WHOLESALE ARRANGEMENT
by Day Leclaire

THE BRIDE *needed* the Groom.
THE GROOM *wanted* the Bride.
BUT THE WEDDING was *more* than
a convenient solution!

Available this month in
The Bridal Collection
Only Make-Believe
by Bethany Campbell
Harlequin Romance #3230

Available wherever Harlequin books are sold.

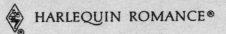

HARLEQUIN ROMANCE®

is

 contemporary
and up-to-date

 heartwarming

 romantic

 exciting

 involving

 fresh and
delightful

 a short, satisfying
read

 wonderful!!

**Today's Harlequin
Romance—the traditional
choice!**

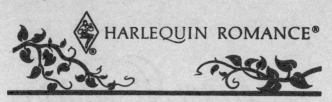

HARLEQUIN ROMANCE®

After her father's heart attack, Stephanie Bloomfield comes home to Orchard Valley, Oregon, to be with him and with her sisters.

Orchard Valley

Steffie learns that many things have changed in her absence—but not her feelings for journalist Charles Tomaselli. He was the reason she left Orchard Valley. Now, three years later, will he give her a reason to stay?

"The Orchard Valley trilogy features three delightful, spirited sisters and a trio of equally fascinating men. The stories are rich with the romance, warmth of heart and humor readers expect, and invariably receive, from Debbie Macomber."

—Linda Lael Miller

Don't miss the Orchard Valley trilogy by Debbie Macomber:

VALERIE   Harlequin Romance #3232 (November 1992)
STEPHANIE   Harlequin Romance #3239 (December 1992)
NORAH   Harlequin Romance #3244 (January 1993)

Look for the special cover flash on each book!

Available wherever Harlequin books are sold.   ORC-2

Back by Popular Demand

Janet Dailey
Americana

Janet Dailey takes you on a romantic tour of America through fifty favorite Harlequin Presents novels, each one set in a different state and researched by Janet and her husband, Bill.

A journey of a lifetime. The perfect collectible series!

December titles

#45 VERMONT
Green Mountain Man
#46 VIRGINIA
Tidewater Lover